The monkey's tale

To: Ji Sho
From: Setarwa

With ever growing
respect & affection,
January, 1999

Peter Bonnici

The monkey's tale

Based on the great epic *Ramayana*

with illustrations by
Dean John Kendrick

STORY
TELLER
TALES

A STORYTELLER TALE
from
THE GOOD COMPANY FOR CHILDREN CO LTD

Storyteller Tales

Published by

The Good Company for Children Co Ltd
3 Parklands Close
off Fife Road
East Sheen
London SW14 7EH

Tel: 0181-876 0445   Fax: 0181-876 0173

First published by The Good Company for Children Co in 1995

ISBN 1-900197-00-6
Copyright © Peter Bonnici 1995

Printed by BPC Wheatons Exeter

Cover design
Quadrant Design Studios, 84 Long Lane, Borough, London SE1

Cover illustration
Dean John Kendrick

Once upon a time...

STORYTELLING is as old as children. From the earliest days, mothers, fathers, uncles, aunts, grandparents and friends have set children on the lap and told tales which happened once upon a time.

The storyteller is an artist, painting pictures in the mind, leading the child across a canvas which bursts with colour at each turn of the story. For sheer fun for both adult and child, nothing can beat the telling of a thunderously good tale.

We at the *Good Company for Children Co Ltd* are delighted to be playing our part in rekindling the art of storytelling. In the process, our aim is to provide great enjoyment and educational value to all who meet our books.

We have tried to make the task of storytelling easier for both reader and listener alike. The books are divided into short episodes, and our hope is that both adult and child will want to carry on with the tale tomorrow. The italicised typeface helps the reader's eye move more easily to pick up the parts where the storyteller's voice would change with each character. Of course those with more practice at telling tales will know the value of silence between dramatic movements.

Storytelling is basically natural to every mother, father, 'aunt' and 'uncle'. Our reasons for publishing are to provide you with the best of company for yourself and children and, we hope, many hours of family happiness along the way.

DAVID BODDY
Publisher
Good Company for Children Co Ltd

The storyteller

MOST PEOPLE look at me and see a monkey — they toss me nuts and oranges. That's why they will never know me as I really am.

The secret truth is, I am Hanumaan, son of the mighty Lord of Wind and Air. I first took birth several thousand years ago with one very important task to do — to help the glorious Prince Raama destroy the power of the Dark Force on earth.

I became Chief Minister to the King of Monkeys and was given a bright and spacious room in his magnificent palace. Life was sweet there — after all it was in an age when most people were honourable and good.

But my special task set me aside from others. While the monkeys and bears in the royal household spent their time eating honey and sipping nectar, I wandered among the trees and felt the kiss of air on my cheeks and hands.

It was then that I realised I could leap. I would soar higher than the mountain tops, carried by my father the Wind, higher than the condor, higher than the tiniest dust mote. In the twinkle of an eye I could leap across whole continents . . . but I won't spoil the story by telling you of my most famous leap yet.

By the way, I, Hanumaan, am the storyteller of the adventures of Raama and Seeta. I first told their story to a group of great apes and bears as we sat huddled together on a chilly beach on the southernmost tip of the country. At the end of another age, I told the story to my brother Prince Bhima, filling him with courage on the eve of the battle that destroyed the whole warrior race.

Now I am back. Yet another age has begun; another person needs to hear the story.

Listen . . .

Guide to pronunciation

THE NAMES in this book have been spelt in such a way as to make it easier to read them out loud. What follows is a guide to pronunciation, spelling each name as it is usually transliterated from the original Sanskrit, then as it sounds closest in English.

The italics indicate which syllable should be emphasised. In order to get the right emphasis, the easiest thing to do is to make sure that the 'light' syllables are very light indeed.

Double vowels indicate the length of the sound.

Usual spelling	In text	Pronunciation
Ashoka	Ashoka	Ash-*oak*-a
Ayodhya	Ayodhya	A-*yo*-dya
Bharata	Bharata	*Bha*-ra-ta
Dandaka	Dandaka	*Dan*-da-ka (to sound like dun-ducker)
Hanuman	Hanumaan	Ha-noo-*maan*
Himalayas	Himaalayas	Hi-*maa*-la-yas (not himma-layers)
Indrajit	Indrajit	*Ind*-ra-jit
Janaka	Janaka	Ja-na-ka
Jatayu	Jataayu	Ja-*taa*-yoo
Lakshmana	Lakshmana	*Laksh*-ma-na (to sound like luck)
Lanka	Lanka	*Lan*-ka (to sound like sunk rather than sank)
Rama	Raama	*Raa*-ma (to sound like Parma)
Ravana	Raavana	*Raa*-va-na
Shatrugna	Shatrugna	Sha-*troog*-na
Sita	Seeta	*See*-ta (to sound like Rita)
Sugriva	Sugreeva	Soo-*gree*-va
Tara	Taara	*Taa*-ra
Vali	Vaali	*Vaa*-li (to sound like Bali)
Vibishana	Vibeeshana	Vi-*bee*-sha-na

Contents

		Page
First day	Meeting Hanumaan	11
Day 2	The King's sacrifice	18
Day 3	The first adventure	26
Day 4	Raama meets Seeta	35
Day 5	The black day	45
Day 6	Banished to the forest	53
Day 7	The good brother	61
Day 8	Adventures in the forest	68
Day 9	The she-demon	76
Day 10	The Dark Force attacks	84
Day 11	Raavana's evil plan	91
Day 12	Raavana kidnaps Seeta	98
Day 13	Raama meets Hanumaan	105
Day 14	Raama helps Sugreeva	113
Day 15	The search begins	121
Day 16	Hanumaan finds Seeta	130
Day 17	Hanumaan on fire	138
Day 18	Raama in Lanka	146
Day 19	War begins	153
Day 20	The battle continues	161
Last day	Winning the peace	169

First day
Meeting Hanumaan

IT WAS ON A DAY pretty much like this one, only warmer and sunnier, that the two children went with Aunt Sissey to play in the park.

"I read somewhere that the secret of a happy family life is exercise and a non-fatty diet," said Aunt Sissey. "What you two need is plenty of fresh air and stretching exercises."

Aunt Sissey was the sort of aunt whose nose was always in a magazine and whose hair was always in a mess. As she spoke two sycamore helicopters silently twirled down on the wind and landed in her hair. They looked like tiny horns. The children laughed behind their hands.

"What are you two little demons plotting?" said Aunt Sissey, peering over the top of her magazine.

"We were just hoping you'd let us go off to our secret trees," the girl said. "You can see them from here."

Aunt Sissey slid her glasses to the tip of her nose and peered over to the tiny copse of poplars. They looked pretty in the sunlight.

"Can't think why you call them your secret trees: they're plain enough for all to see. Go on, off with you," laughed Aunt Sissey, stretching to give the boy a playful smack with her rolled up magazine. She missed and the children skipped away.

"We'll be perfectly safe," shouted the boy. "Maybe we'll even find some of those sweet-smelling flowers you like."

"Don't be too long," Aunt Sissey called, but the wind carried away her words.

THERE WAS SOMETHING STRANGE about the secret trees this time. The tall dark poplars were full of wind — swaying, hissing, howling, clacking their branches at the children as they approached. The children squeezed their way through the gap in the laurel bushes to the magical circle of grass, hidden from the rest of the park by the ring of trees. In it they became acrobats in a circus or actors on a grassy green stage and they whooped and sang and gave big speeches at the tops of their voices and clapped at each other's performances. No one else seemed to have found this hidden world. The only audience was the birds.

Imagine their surprise this time when, instead of being the only ones there, they saw a large Persian carpet in the middle of the green. On it was one half-eaten orange, three whole ones and the empty shells of many walnuts.

"Something's different," said the girl. "Someone's here."

"Ssh. Listen," said the boy. The wind was powerful now. Dry leaves chased round the circle of trees like mad dogs in a race. No birds. Just the wind. "It sounds like angry wind. I think it's trying to tell us something."

He cupped his hands to his mouth and shouted up to the trees: "Okay, we're listening . . ."

Suddenly, the wind dropped to a whisper and the birds took up their singing once more. The poplars stood still like tall and silent guards again.

"There, you see," said the boy. "I'm lord of the wind!"

The words had no sooner left his lips when the sound of a sharp crack broke the silence. The birds all took off in panic, flying this way and that in a crazy dash to escape. The top of one of the giant poplars began to creak under the strain of something heavy, its leaves rustling, twigs cracking. The girl found the boy's hand and held tight. The fine hairs on the back of her neck tingled.

"What do you think it is?" she whispered. Whatever was in the tree was getting nearer to the ground. Nearer, nearer . . . The children stood stock still. Then they saw it — an enormous dark brown monkey, the size of a bear cub.

He took his time to climb through the lowermost branches, using one hand, both feet and his powerful tail. He jumped the last four feet — more like floating down to the ground it seemed. With his back still to them, he carefully picked off the odd twig from his shoulders and head, dusted down his mighty arms and then rose to his full height.

He turned, stared straight at the children and, with what looked like a smile on his face and light in his eyes, spoke in a gentle voice: "Come and join me in some food. Come, come. I've been expecting someone like you for thousands of years."

The children, still stuck together, holding tight, moved like a stiff four-legged creature to the carpet. "I hope you like oranges," said the monkey. The girl nodded, the boy shook his head.

"Does not like oranges," said the monkey as he lowered himself to sit on the carpet. "I'll try to remember that." He picked up one of the oranges, turned it round and round in cupped palms and then offered it back to the boy. "Try it now," he said.

The boy obeyed silently. "Funny," he said, "I didn't think oranges tasted like this. It's not bad. Did you just do some magic?" He felt the girl tug on his shirt. "I was only asking a question," he said in a huffed whisper. "How many times do you meet a talking monkey, then? He's got to be magic."

The monkey looked as if he was smiling again. He shook his head slowly. "No magic. You just stopped believing you didn't like oranges and, obviously, you tasted the orange as it really tastes. In this time of yours, I suppose you could say it's nothing short of a miracle — people dropping their precious ideas about what they like and what they don't like." Then his mind seemed to leap off to a distant time and his eyes sparkled with pure happiness. "It wasn't like that in the time when I first met them . . ."

"Met who?" asked the girl.

"Raama and Seeta," said the monkey. "He was such a good man . . . she was such a fine woman. They were so full of love that sometimes it was difficult to know which one of them was who."

The children were kneeling on the edge of the carpet now. All fear had long since vanished. A gentle breeze started up. The sun was gentle too. Two sparrows hopped onto the carpet, one of them picking away at the empty walnut shells, the other watching.

"Well . . . ?" said the boy.

"Well what?" said the monkey.

"Well, are you going to tell us more about them?"

"Well . . . Yes, I just might do that. I haven't told this tale for a long, long time. It's right for the telling once more." The monkey sat upright. The children rolled over onto their tummies and took up their favourite position for listening to stories.

Then the monkey began . . .

MANY THOUSAND YEARS AGO, in a time they call the Silver Age, there was a truly magnificent city called Ayodhya in the most splendid kingdom that had ever been seen. The streets were broad and clean, the houses lining them were white and richly decorated with carvings of birds and leaves and animals of every type. There were temples too with domes rising high above the roofs and terraces of the houses, glinting gold in the sunlight. But higher and grander than all these was the palace.

In the streets and market squares below, people went about their business — some selling flowers, others selling fruit, others selling jewels and clothes and toys from all over the world. One man had an enormous cage filled with squawking green parrots that flapped around, knocking off his cap each time he tried to catch one for a customer.

There were no cars or trucks then. Instead there were elephants piled high with multi-coloured carpets, and donkeys laden with sticks of sugar cane and sweet smelling juices, and camels carrying rich silks and hot spices, and horses with warriors mounted proudly.

The sounds that filled the city were happy sounds — people laughing, someone singing. And as you walked past the houses, through the open doors you could hear the voices of children reciting their times tables. Further up, as you got nearer to the palace, the sounds of hustle and bustle gave way to the bells of the temples and the sound of priests reciting their prayers — a sound like bees buzzing and buzzing, rising and falling in waves.

Then finally, you reach the gates of the palace. It is quite silent at first, but gradually, as your listening gets finer, you hear the sound of sparkling water, trickling from one hundred tiny fountains along the pool that led through green lawns all the way to the palace steps.

Peacocks pecked for worms on the lawns, their long tail feathers tucked back tightly, swishing the grass with a sound like silk ball-gowns. Then every so often, one of the peacocks would lift its throat and cry out its piercing call — again and again. It's a sound that reaches the stars.

This is the city into which Raama was destined to be born. It is the city that raised him and loved him. It is the city from which he left to have his grand adventures with his wife Seeta.

THEIRS IS truly a story of love and honour. It is a story of gods and demons, men and monkeys, boons and curses, terrible battles and sweet, sweet peace. In it there is wonderful magic and frightening magic, wise men and dreadful deeds. The earth trembles at times and then gentle rain falls with flowers from the heavens.

It is a timeless story — many, many thousand years old and yet it is as if it only happened yesterday. It belongs to all the world and yet only a few can really hear it. I tell this story from time to time to special people and those who hear it become wiser and stronger. I have waited long to tell it to you . . .

I will tell you this tale of Raama, the most courageous of princes, and Seeta, his wife, the purest of princesses.

You will hear of how, just when they are to be most happy, their happiness is snatched away and they are banished into the wild forest.

I will tell you about their adventures in the forest and of the Lord of the Dark Force and the dreadful day when he steals the princess.

You will hear of Raama's search for his wife and of my part in finding her — yes I was there too.

Then I'll tell of our mighty battle in which thousands died, in which the Lord of the Dark Force is killed and the princess is rescued.

The monkey opened his huge mouth as if he was going to shout out something, but it turned into a wide, wide yawn instead. "It's a long story, this story of Raama and Seeta. And just now, carried on the wind, came the thoughts of your Aunt Sissey. She's getting worried about you. So come back tomorrow."

"What?" said the boy in his most grumpy voice.

"That's not fair," said the girl. "You can't stop now."

"I can. And I will," said the monkey. Then he closed his eyes shut tight.

"But . . ." began the boy.

The monkey raised one black finger. "Tomorrow," he said. "Come back and call me and I will be here."

"How do we call you?" said the girl.

"By my name, of course," said the monkey. "I am Hanumaan, son of the Wind." Slowly he rose from the carpet and walked over to the tallest poplar and climbed into its branches and vanished. The wind started up again.

"Tomorrow!" shouted the boy. "You'd better be there!"

Back in the park the boy and girl walked in silence. A puff of wind blew a lock of the boy's hair into his eyes and he felt something brush against his cheek. There on the grass were three sweet-smelling flowers for Aunt Sissey.

Day 2
The King's sacrifice

AS SOON as they could get away the next day, the children were back in the magic circle of trees. The carpet and the oranges were there, and this time there was also a bowl of sweets; but no monkey.

"Monkey, monkey, here boy," called the boy. Nothing happened. He whistled. "Here monkey. Monkey. Come on." Nothing happened. In a rage he kicked one of the oranges right into the bushes.

"I told you he wasn't real," he said to the girl.

"He's certainly not a dog," she said. "He told us his name."

"What was it?"

They both fell silent. The wind started to stir. It made a sound of wind in grass, in branches, in a bamboo forest, on the sea.

"Ooooo ... ooooo," hooted the boy.

"That's it," cried the girl, "Han-oooo-maan. Han-oooo-maan!" they called and Hanumaan appeared at the top of the tall poplar.

"You're back for more," he called down. "For a moment, I thought it was someone else — someone who'd lost their dog — maybe a footballer or someone like that."

The boy remembered kicking the orange. When Hanumaan wasn't looking he rushed over to the bushes and found it. It was truly in a sorry state for an orange. Hanumaan glanced slyly up at him. "I see you've already begun peeling your orange. You must have started to like them, eh?"

"Hmmm. Delicious," said the boy, biting into the soft juicy fruit. And, you know what, it really was delicious!

"Just imagine," said the monkey as they all took their place on the carpet, "how many years you've wasted not liking oranges." He cleared his throat. "Still ... it's nothing like as many years I've been around. Shut your eyes and let your listening take you back to the beginning. Are you ready ... ?"

THE KING'S PALACE was the jewel in the city of
Ayodhya, with flags and turrets, lawns and lotus ponds,
gardens and underground passages. The massive kitchens
downstairs were a bustle of goings and comings, fat butchers
and rosy-cheeked pastry maids, live turtles and game birds,
and mountains of vegetables. The cooks had their jobs well
cut out, because no sooner had they finished preparing one
banquet than it was time for the chopping and washing to
begin for the next meal. From the kitchen rose up the most
delicious smells of cooking that made all mouths water.

Above the kitchens there were one thousand rooms, full of
beautiful furniture and long silk wall-coverings and large
bathing pools. These too were busy places with maids and
menservants making beds and fetching sweets and generally
making life happy for those in court.

The ladies in court were chosen for their brightness —
always flowers in their hair, always beautiful necklaces and
gold bangles, with voices like angels and minds that could
unravel deep mysteries — but even brighter than all these
was the light in their eyes.

The men of court were upright and noble. They
understood the messages in the stars and the art of warfare.
They knew the holy teachings and the beauty of geometry.

Finally there was the throne room with a simple throne for
the King and three seats beside it — one for each of his wives
— and a fine carpet for his wise Counsellor. The king of this
magnificent city was pleased with the happiness of all around
him, but in his heart he was sad.

"Our city is fair and its people are wealthy," he said to his
old teacher. *"We are blessed by rich lands and plenty of food. We
have no enemies."*

19

"Then what hangs so heavy on your heart?" said the wise Counsellor.

"I have three wives," said the King, *"but no children. Who will rule after me and keep our city safe?"*

"I have been waiting for you to say these words, Your Majesty," the Counsellor said. *"Each month I watch the movements of the planets to find out when is best for children. The time is now right — a bright new star has moved into the heavens above the city. Tomorrow we should start preparations for an offering to the gods. And if they are pleased with your offering, they might grant you your wish for children."*

The very next day preparations began. Thousands of people attended the ceremonies. Priests travelled in from forests and mountains all over the kingdom. Monks left their caves, wise men left their followers. *"The King is making an offering for the sake of children,"* the word went out.

All in the kingdom wanted this to be the most perfect event because they wanted the king to be happy. So mothers made sure their children had a bath every day, that their hair was brushed, their clothes were clean. Even in the market square you could see cats licking their kittens and in the fields large white birds picked the nits off the heads of water buffalo. Men brought themselves under control and looked tall and walked like lords and remembered the simple, natural ways of old.

NOW IT MUST BE SAID, that the people of the city were not the only ones who were interested in what was going on. In the heavens too the gods had gathered for a meeting. They were worried about things on earth. People seemed to be frightened of something and had stopped praying. They had even stopped giving offerings to the gods. The reason for all this was that the power of the Dark Force on earth had grown — with a terrible army of Night Rangers that threatened all those who worshipped the gods.

The mighty leader of the Night Rangers was called Raavana. He had been a good man once. In fact he had been so good that, as a reward, the ruler of the gods promised to grant him any wish he wanted. Raavana thanked the gods for their boon and said: *"I wish to be so powerful that no god or demon can kill me."* His wish was granted. That's when things began to go wrong.

At first he did simple bad acts like using bad language. Then it got worse — he became cruel to people and finally he started killing good men and women and children.

"How can we stop him?" people asked. They prayed to the gods to stop the wicked ways of Raavana, but the gods could not harm him because he was protected by his boon. Soon a huge army of the Dark Force gathered round Raavana and he became their king. They made life on earth very miserable — and little could be done about it.

So, the gods had a meeting to ask how could they stop the wickedness spread by Raavana. No one knew the answer. Then the Lord Protector of Men spoke: *"The boon of Raavana means that no god or demon can kill him. But the boon does not save him from men or animals."*

A ripple of excitement ran through the heavens. (On earth this was felt as a gentle shower of rose petals.) The gods looked down to earth and saw the preparations under way for the King's offering for children. They turned to the Lord Protector and pleaded: *"Please be born to the King who is about to make an offering for children. Then, once you have taken on human form, you can put a stop to the evil ways of Raavana."*

The Lord Protector of Men smiled: *"And you will be safe up here in heaven watching the fun, I suppose."*

At that moment a mighty hurricane blew through the gathering, scattering flowers all over, blowing clothes into faces, messing up neatly combed hair. The Lord of the Wind had arrived. *"I am happy to play my part in helping to defeat the Dark Force. I too can be born on earth."*

"The Lord of the Wind! That's your father, isn't it?" said the girl.

Hanumaan nodded.

"If that's your father, then how come you're only a monkey?" said the boy.

The bristles on Hanumaan's shoulders stood up like great black spears. He looked enormous, and dark as a thunder cloud. His eyes glowed red as the sun over the desert. The boy became frightened.

But the girl reached out a pale trembling hand and stroked Hanumaan's powerful arms. "Please forgive us for being so rude. We see a monkey, not the son of a god," she said. And Hanumaan returned to his gentle form and began to pick at the sweets in the bowl.

The girl nudged the boy with her elbow. "Say something," she hissed.

The boy slowly stood up straight and tall before Hanumaan. "Forgive me, sir, for speaking to you as just a monkey. I'll try never to forget who you truly are."

Without looking up at him Hanumaan nodded and stretched out his long dark arm and offered the boy a sweet. "You can call me Hanumaan," he said in a gentle voice.

"Thank you, sir," said the boy. "But, if you please, if it isn't too rude a question, would you explain how you come to have this shape?"

"My father felt that if the Lord Protector of Men was going to be born as a man, then it was not proper that he should be born as a man too. So he chose to be born as an animal — after all Raavana wasn't safe from animals either!" said Hanumaan. "And all the other gods decided to follow his example. Some chose to be born as monkeys, others chose to become bears, some to become vultures. That's what was agreed and that's what happened. So can the story continue now?"

The children nodded. "Yes please, Hanumaan."

THE DAY FINALLY ARRIVED for the King's ceremony. It was a grand affair, lasting many days. The gods were well pleased with the offering. The Lord Protector of Men prepared a bowl of heavenly food full of his power for the King's wives. A shining ball of light came down from the skies. It circled the field trailing soft glowing droplets on the crowd. The people were washed by light, their skin tingled, their eyes brightened, their hair glowed.

Then the ball of light touched the ground in front of the King. It bobbed gently for a moment and then, with a puff, it vanished. There, at the King's feet was a golden bowl with the special food. The wise Counsellor, who knew the secrets of the heavens and the ways of the gods, told the king that he should share the food between his wives.

The first queen was given half the food. She ate it slowly, tasting every mouthful. It danced on her tongue and filled her nostrils with its delicate scent. The second queen was given half of what remained and she too ate with delight. The third queen was given half of what then remained, leaving some food still in the bowl. The King gave the third queen a second helping and the bowl was empty.

Soon after eating this heavenly food, the three queens gave birth to sons. The first queen's son was called Raama and he had half the power of the Lord Protector of Men. The other half of the power was shared between the children of the

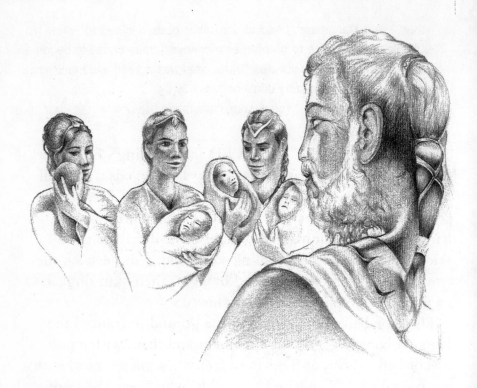

other queens. The second queen's son was called Bharata. The third queen had twins, one called Lakshmana and the other called Shatrugna, because she had eaten two helpings.

No one realised that these princes of Ayodhya were really the Lord Protector of Men being born on earth. And no one was aware of the secret army of monkeys and bears being born in the forests and hills all over the kingdom at the same time.

The Lords of Heaven had taken their places on earth. Their plan to defeat Raavana had begun . . .

Hanumaan yawned, stretched out on the carpet and fell instantly asleep. The children looked at one another in astonishment, looked at the snoring monkey, reluctantly got up, gathered together the orange peels and made their way quietly to the secret entrance to the grove.

"I don't suppose we should try to wake him to say thank you and ask if he's going to be here tomorrow," said the boy.

"I don't think we could wake him if we tried," said the girl.

The boy nodded. "If he really has been waiting a thousand years for us, I'm not surprised he conks out like that. But I can hardly wait to hear how they killed that Raavana."

Day 3
The first adventure

GETTING TO THE PARK the next day was a bit of an adventure for the children. They told Aunt Sissey that they were going to play with their friends next door, but carried on towards the park which was just at the bottom of the road.

This made the girl feel edgy. Everything they met seemed to swoop down on them like Night Rangers. First it was a rumbling black truck, spraying hot tar across the road. The boy said that it was the blood of Raavana pouring through the hundred wounds from the arrows in battle. The girl told him to shut up and hurry.

"I don't really like doing this," said the girl. "Aunt Sissey thinks we're next door." Suddenly two boys on mountain bikes swooped round the corner almost knocking the children into the bushes.

"That's it," said the girl, "we can't stay."

Hanumaan was already waiting when they arrived at the secret trees. His eyes lit up when he saw them. But before he uttered one word, the girl said: "We're just here to tell you that we can't come every day. So thank you for your story, but we must get back now." Her breath came in small puffs, her face felt quite hot.

Hanumaan smiled. "Your words have just killed one of the Night Rangers — the Dishonest Demon," he said. "Well done." Then he cupped his hands into a ball, blew into it and tossed the breath to the children. "That's the next bit of story ... it's only the length of one breath, I'm afraid. Call me when it runs out." He joined his palms flat and raised them above his head and with one leap was at the top of the tree.

"See what you just did," said the boy.

"Come on, we're going home," said the girl.

As they walked, Hanumaan's voice grew in their ears ...

THE CITY OF AYODHYA was in celebration when news spread of the birth of the four princes. Music played late at night. There were fireworks and parties in the streets. Old enemies shook hands like friends, children had the whole week off school, men built huge stars of bamboo and silk and hung them over the streets. Women created the most beautiful decorations on their doorsteps with coloured powders but the wind blew them away at night; the women made them again the next day.

The King and his three queens proudly watched their sons grow in this beautiful city. The princes were taught all the skills of riding and archery. They studied the holy books and heard the tales of far away places. The wise Counsellor at court made sure that their studies were of the finest, the music they heard was of the finest, the food they ate was the finest. The people of the city loved the princes; but most of all they loved the eldest, Raama.

Raama was brave and tall and had hair as black as a raven's wing. His speech was soft and his words were wise, even though he was still a young boy. His brother Lakshmana, one of the twins, loved him a lot too. They would always go riding together and always spoke of the adventures they would have when they grew up.

LITTLE DID THEY KNOW that the first adventure was just round the corner. It started like this:

One evening, just as the court was about to have their meal, there came a heavy knocking on the door. Before them stood the most powerful sage of the land, a man of great wisdom, who had managed to steady his mind in truth.

People were frightened of him because of the power of his magic — once he even started to create a new universe, but the gods begged him to stop and he did. So you can imagine the scene in the palace. People fell to their knees. Even the King bowed before him.

"It is an honour that you should enter my home," said the King and, as was the custom of the time, offered to feed the sage.

"I'm not here for food," came back the reply.

"Ask for anything," said the King, *"whatever you came for, I will give you."*

The sage looked the King straight in his eyes. *"My hermitage needs help. Each evening, as we are about to make our offerings to the gods, two Night Rangers, full of the Dark Force, fly into the room, screeching and howling and using all sorts of curses and pour blood over the sacred fire to spoil everything."*

"I will send my best soldiers," said the king. *"They will protect you."*

"Bah! Soldiers! What can they do against the Dark Force?" said the sage.

"Then tell me how I can help and your wish will be granted," promised the King.

"Give me your son Raama to kill these evil creatures," said the sage.

The King was stunned at the request and begged the sage to ask for someone else to help — after all, Raama was not yet sixteen years old. But the more the king tried to get out of his promise, the more angry the sage became. Smoke started to rise from his clothes, and sparks started to fly from his staff.

Finally the King said: *"Don't be angry. Understand that*

Raama is my eldest son and I fear that he will be no match for Raavana's Dark Force. But a king's word is his bond."

EARLY NEXT DAY, when the morning mists hung over the earth like a pale silken bedspread, Raama and his younger brother Lakshmana left the city with the sage. With their bows and arrows, spears and swords, the princes looked like brave warriors, not young boys. The princes were in a solemn mood — heads erect, each footstep steady and firm. And with each step they filled with courage.

Their journey brought them to a dark forest in which the soil was black, the trees were black, the clouds were black. It looked as if the forest had been destroyed in a fire. Nothing living remained. A few vultures fighting over the body of a dead calf stopped for a moment to watch the princes. Lakshmana tried to shoo them off, but they just hopped a few paces, spreading their twisted wings, and then returned to their meal.

"I have seen many places in my father's kingdom," said Raama, *"they have been beautiful and brought happiness to the hearts of all who saw them. In all that time, I have never once seen a place like this."*

"This forest was also beautiful once. The soil had been made rich by sacred waters falling from the heavens. But an evil witch and her son moved in and destroyed all that," said the sage. *"They killed the animals, they frightened the villagers and they ruined the soil by pouring their evil into it."*

"Why doesn't someone get rid of her?" said Lakshmana.

"They are all afraid," said the sage. *"But you two can help these people by killing the witch."*

"My father taught us that it is wrong to harm a woman," said Raama. *"Can't we just frighten her away?"*

"Be on your guard," said the sage to the two princes. *"She kills all those who enter here. Show her no mercy."*

The words had no sooner left his lips than there came a blood-curdling shriek from the skies and the princes were showered with foul-smelling mud. Raama dropped to one knee and in a flash he had three arrows shooting towards the sound. A huge dark shape flew at him, knocking him off balance.

"There she is," yelled Lakshmana.

Hiding among the trees was an enormous woman, eyes bulging, the veins on her forehead standing out, rotting teeth being shown by a cruel snarl. She kicked up black dust and hurled a shower of boulders at Raama.

A stream of arrows shot from his bow, reducing the boulders to dust. This made the witch furious. She tore up a tree by its roots and charged at the princes.

Two crescent-shaped arrows sliced off her arms and the tree fell harmlessly to the ground. Taraka the witch opened her vile mouth and screamed. From it streamed poisonous snakes and black mud.

"Kill her," shouted the sage

"But she's a woman," cried Raama.

"Kill her," shouted the sage again.

Arrows sparked from Raama's bow and pierced the black heart of the witch. With a howl she fell to the ground and died.

A fine shower of rain fell from the heavens. The earth gave up her fresh scent again and life slowly started to appear once more. The vultures took one look at the princes and hurried off. A family of birds, singing sweetly, flew over and circled the forest.

The sage was overjoyed with the bravery of the two princes. *"Tonight,"* he said, *"you will receive a precious gift."*

He led them through the forest which was now bursting with life as they walked. Soon they arrived at the banks of a sacred river where they made camp for the night. When the sun was setting and they had said their prayers and sharpened their weapons, the sage stood with arms outstretched and said: *"Now."*

It was silent at first and then a low rumble came from the belly of the clouds. They parted with a flash of lightning and, streaming from the heavens, was the most magnificent army of shining weapons: daggers, knives, shafts, swords, maces, spears — each one more beautiful than the one before. One by one, they swooped from the sky, bowed to the princes, whispered their secret name and said: *"Call my name and I will be with you in battle."*

The princes were dazzled by the sheer brilliance of what they had seen as the last of the weapons flew back into the clouds. They turned to thank the sage, but he stopped their words with a raised hand. *"It's not over yet,"* he said.

Then the ground started to tremble, the sky flashed yellow and electric blue and green, wild animals shot for cover and slowly ... ever so slowly ... the clouds parted once more and the most fearsome weapon appeared before them. Lakshmana fell to the ground and covered his eyes. Raama didn't move. The mighty weapon hovered three feet in front of him, studying the young prince: *"I am the Brahmaa-astra, Weapon of the Lord Creator. I have never been beaten in battle. Nothing escapes me. I carry all enemies into the jaws of death."*

Then it bowed to Raama and said, *"I am your humble servant, brave Raama. Call my name and I will appear ready to help."* With that, the *Brahmaa-astra* flashed back and vanished.

"This is excellent, excellent," said the sage, *"more than could be hoped for."* He patted Raama on the back. *"Consider yourself truly honoured, my son."*

THE NEXT EVENING at the hermitage of the sage, the two princes were greeted like heroes. The monks had already heard about how the witch had been killed and of how the princes received magic weapons — they felt safe again.

"Let's not waste time in idle chatter," said the sage. *"The moment approaches for the Dark Force to make its play."*

His warning was most timely — the sky opened and thick blood showered down on the monks. *"They're here!"* shouted Raama.

Lakshmana whipped an arrow into his bow string and the two princes stood rock steady. More blood showered down followed by mad, howling, shrieking laughter as two Night Rangers flew down from the darkness. Arrows snaked across the starless night sky and stunned them in their flight. They turned and swooped down again. Raama let fly an arrow with a tip shaped like the new moon. It caught one of the Night Rangers by the neck and carried him thousands of miles and dumped him in the sea. His friend met the same fate.

But then the sky filled with hundreds of black figures who swooped down like bats at the princes. Raama and Lakshmana moved at the speed of summer lightning, arrows flashing from their bows lighting up the sky which soon filled with humming, screaming, howling, gurgling as one

by one the army of the Dark Force fell to the forest floor.
Dead.

That night you can imagine the celebration. Large bonfires
were built and sweet smelling powders tossed onto them. The
beautiful offering reached right up to the heavens. The gods
showered down flowers on Raama and Lakshmana and the
powerful sage hugged them like sons. *"Tomorrow will be the
last day of our journey together,"* he said. *"We will go to the
kingdom of the wise king Janaka and his beautiful daughter
Seeta."*

"Sleep, sleep deeply tonight ... for tomorrow you will find peace."
That night the children fell fast and deeply asleep.

Day 4
Raama meets Seeta

THE GIRL WOKE HAPPY. She shook her sleeping brother. "Do you want to hear my dream?" she said.

He pulled the duvet over his head and said: "I want to sleep."

But she told him anyway: "I was very, very tiny — like one drop of a spray of scent — deep down in the earth. And yet all the forests and oceans and suns and sounds and thoughts and darkness were in me. I was brilliant."

"And as you grew, you became more and more like a human baby," added a familiar voice from behind.

The children spun round. "Hanumaan!" they both cried in delight. But there was no Hanumaan there — just a breeze blowing the curtains of their bedroom.

But Hanumaan's voice seemed to be all around them. "That tiny particle of scent was how Seeta began life in the depths of the earth. There she grew, till one day, when a good and wise king called Janaka was ploughing his sacred field, the earth opened up and gave him the beautiful baby girl."

"The Earth was Seeta's mother?" exclaimed the girl.

"Anyone who believes that someone's mother is the Earth is really silly," said the boy.

Then, just as the children were about to begin a fight, Hanumaan's voice boomed in their ears: "RAAMA ... RAAMA ..." In a flash, their minds became quite quiet. The beautiful sound continued, gently now ...

RAAMA AND HIS BROTHER set out the next morning with the wise sage to the kingdom of Seeta's father. The monks gathered to see them off, showering blessing and garlands on the two princes. Birds and animals of the forest followed them to the end of the forest path and watched the two princes and their teacher disappear over the brow of the purple hills and enter Janaka's kingdom.

The city reminded Raama of home. Here too people seemed happy because they had a wise and happy king. Flags flew from the rooftops and large colourful birds could be seen everywhere. News of the adventures of the two young princes had already reached the city and a crowd of young men followed the princes, asking Raama if they could carry his bow and asking Lakshmana if they could carry his spear. By the time they reached the palace walls, the two princes, stripped of all their weapons, looked like people from the city and the young men who followed them looked like warriors.

Princess Seeta and her handmaidens rushed to the ramparts to see what was happening. They too had heard of the bravery of Raama and had bets about who could spot him first. The maidens all chose different young men, tricked by the weapons they carried, but Seeta wasn't fooled for a minute.

"He's the one who walks silently, looking neither left nor right," she said. *"His back is straight, his shoulders and arms powerful, his hair the colour of night, his eyes the shape of lotus petals. Around him is light. His feet don't seem to touch the ground."*

"Your feet seem to have left the ground as well," teased one of her friends.

"He's too skinny," teased another.

"We'll see who's right," smiled Seeta and they all rushed back into the palace to get a better look at what happened next.

KING JANAKA GREETED his visitors in the large

circular hall of the palace. Seeta and her friends watched from a balcony high up.

The King bowed before the wise sage, touching his feet.

"*This is Raama,*" said the sage, "*Prince of Ayodhya, killer of demons, friend of the good, destroyer of the Night Rangers that trouble our land. And beside him is his faithful brother, Prince Lakshmana, brave warrior and good friend.*"

King Janaka said: "*News of your adventures has already reached our ears and we are honoured that you should join us on this special day. Today, the most powerful warriors from the whole world have gathered here to try to win the hand of my daughter Seeta.*"

Raama recognised some of those who had come for the contest and had heard of the bravery of some others. This was truly a powerful gathering of men in a truly magnificent palace. Raama's eyes studied the gold drapes and magnificent carpets and carved columns in white marble studded with precious stones of green and wine red. Tier upon tier of balconies circled the main hall, rising all the way up to the glass dome at the top through which sunlight streamed.

Finally his eyes rested on the group of young girls who were laughing and pointing.

One of them was more beautiful than all the others, the sunlight warming her black hair and glinting off her jewellery, light flashing from her brown eyes and open smile. Shyly, she waved a tiny white handkerchief at Raama and then blushed and covered her face. Immediately a sense of peace and happiness filled Raama's heart. He turned to King Janaka and said: "*If your majesty permits, I would like to join the contest too.*"

"*Young man, I not only permit it,*" said the King, "*but I insist that you try for the hand of Seeta.*" And at that moment something fluttered down through the shaft of sunlight like a nervous butterfly and landed at Raama's feet. It was the tiny white handkerchief. He picked it up and put it to his nose, breathed in the delicate scent and he became still.

"*Let the contest begin,*" said the King and a space cleared in the large circular hall. Seeta was called down to sit beside her father.

Men, women and children from the city, dressed in their finest clothes, crowded in and lined the circular balconies, calling out for their favourites to win. One woman shouted: "*Come on, Raama! You can do it!*"

And Seeta shut her eyes and whispered: "*Yes, yes, yes please win Raama.*"

THE KING CLAPPED TWICE. The large doors to the palace opened. A huge cart, pulled by five hundred soldiers, rumbled its way into the centre of the hall, the shaft of sunlight falling on a large iron box on the cart. Eight strong men were required to open the iron box to reveal a mighty golden bow that dazzled the eyes by its glory.

The Chief Minister banged his staff three times and announced: "*This is the mighty bow of the gods, given as a gift to our good King Janaka. The King has promised that the man who can shoot an arrow from this bow will win the hand of his daughter Seeta in marriage. Let the contestants step forward.*"

The sound of excitement rippled through the crowd as the bravest and strongest of warrior princes pushed their way to the front. They looked truly magnificent in their fine clothes and wonderful armour. Standing beside them, dressed in his simple forest wear, was Raama.

A hush descended on the hall as the first of the princes stepped onto the cart. He was a big fat fellow with a huge black moustache and bushy eyebrows. He took one look at the bow, nodded and gave a proud smile. He raised one arm to the king and grabbed the bow. He struggled to lift it. And he grunted and puffed and strained, his face getting red, the veins on his neck and forehead bulging with the effort. The crowd cheered him on. *"Go for it!" "Lift it!"* But the mighty bow didn't move an inch. Finally, exhausted, he fell back to the ground defeated.

The next contestant eagerly rushed forward, jumped onto the cart and tried to lift the bow. But he too failed. And then the next and the next and the next. After all the princes had had their turn and lay puffing and groaning and sweating on the ground, Raama stepped forward.

He looked tiny compared to the others, but he leapt nimbly onto the cart. The crowd fell silent. There was no movement in Raama's face or eyes. He glanced up at Seeta and then even the movements in his heart came to rest.

With palms joined, he bowed to the mighty bow and said: *"O powerful gift from the gods, you who have defeated many in battle, and many in this hall, please forgive me if I seem rude in trying to lift you when so many have failed. Instead, lend me victory."*

Then Raama lifted the mighty bow as if it was as light as a feather, stood it upright, placed one end against his toe, bent it back and strung it. Then, drawing an arrow from his quiver, he held it against the string, pointed the bow straight up to the heavens and pulled back on the string and pulled and pulled. The arrow flew. Then . . . CRACK! . . . like the sound of angry thunder, the mighty bow snapped in two.

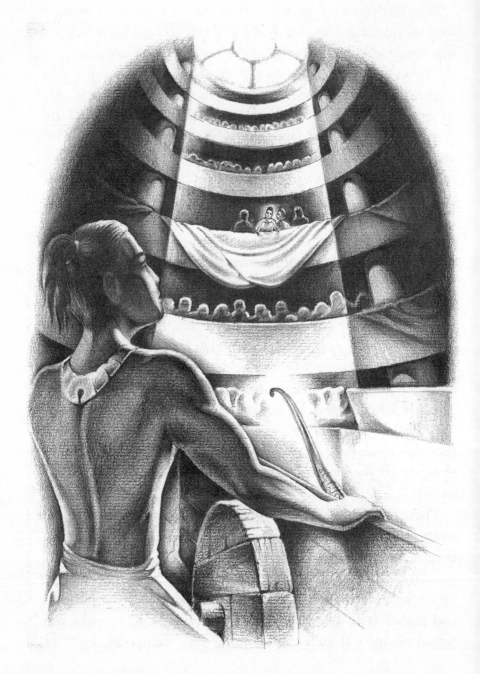

A huge cheer went up from the crowd. Banners streamed down on the young prince. Even the gods in the heavens cried out: *Excellent! Excellent!* and showered down flowers over Raama. Seeta was the happiest person in the hall. Lakshmana was jumping up and down, whooping: *"Raama! Raama!"* and the crowd took up the chant: *RAAMA! RAAMA!* the sound filling the city, reaching the stars, entering all hearts.

MESSENGERS WERE SENT immediately to pass on the good news to Raama's parents. Soon preparations were well under way for the biggest wedding that the land had ever seen. Kings and queens, lords and ladies came from the four corners of the known world. Special fields were planted with lawns and builders began work erecting homes for all the visitors. More food was brought in on camels, more flowers, more drink, more of this and more of that — in fact more of everything was required. Thousands of guests had been invited.

Raama and Lakshmana were given special rooms in the palace and fine clothes to wear. The lords and ladies of the court felt proud to have two such heroes living amongst them and each of them tried to appear as if they were special friends of the brothers.

At the parties in the evening, the ladies all queued up to dance for Lakshmana. Raama, of course, had Seeta as his constant companion.

The men of the court insisted on going hunting with the princes or having long talks with them. Then they would go to their friends and say: *"Why, just yesterday, when I was hunting with Raama, he told me that my horse was the most splendid he had ever seen."* Or: *"Lakshmana told me that my painting of his portrait was magnificent!"*

Raama ignored all this flattery and spent most of his time with Seeta. She took him to her favourite places in the palace grounds. She showed him the secret rose garden with hundreds and hundreds of roses of all sorts of colours from deep black to shining blue, dark red to orange, yellow to the brightest pink.

Raama picked a beautiful pink rose and placed it against Seeta's cheek. *"Beside your beauty, my princess, this rose is no more than a common weed."*

"Stop teasing me," said Seeta, blushing deeply.

"Raama does not know how to tell a lie," said Raama.

Seeta took his hand and showed him her other favourite places: the tree house beside the lily pond; the swing covered with dandelions and vines; the family of leopard cubs that ran up to her like kittens and fed from her hand; the secret hide-away where she and her sisters escaped to when they knew they were in trouble.

Raama loved following his princess around the palace. And he too showed off a bit. One day he shot a target blindfolded and then shot a second arrow into the shaft of the first and a third arrow into the second, and he kept on shooting till ten arrows had left his bow.

Seeta clapped. *"That's wonderful,"* she cried.

"That's nothing," said Raama, who then proceeded to show off even more of his skills.

At night they walked together under an enormous black sky, studded with stars and lit by pin-pricks of light from a million fire-flies. Raama pointed out the various planets and told Seeta their names and how they shaped the lives of people on earth.

He pointed to one bright star and said: *"When that star is directly above our heads, the time will be right for our wedding day."*

"Let's hope it hurries up," said Seeta.

"It will," said Raama.

WHEN RAAMA'S FATHER finally arrived at Janaka's palace with his three queens and his other two sons, he was astonished to see the beauty of the work that had gone into creating such a glorious city for the visitors.

King Janaka greeted Raama's parents as if they were long lost family. He took one look at Raama together with his brothers and said to their father: *"Why have just one wedding when you have four magnificent sons and I have four fine daughters. Let our families be truly joined as one."* And that's what happened. It was a magnificent event.

There was not a single person who wasn't happy. Even those who were ill became well. Everyone was full of life and energy. There was peace and happiness and bliss everywhere.

The door of the children's bedroom suddenly burst open and Aunt Sissey staggered in, panting. "So there you are," she said. "I suppose you were hiding from all that wind, my poor little lambs."

The children just stared at her.

"Well, didn't you hear it? Shutters slamming, chickens blown all over the yard. I didn't know what was going on. The funny thing was that it was only this house that seemed to be affected. Anyway, as long as you're okay."

The children continued to stare in silence. Aunt Sissey sighed. The wind suddenly stopped. All was silent once more. Then, rising out of the silence, came the high pitched whine of a wasp . . .

"Something bad's going to happen," thought the girl.

Day 5
The black day

THE CHILDREN were allowed to go to the park the next day. The afternoon sky filled with dark clouds that threatened a storm, the wind whipped up paper and dust in a fury as if battle had already begun. When the children reached the secret grove where they had first met Hanumaan, the tall poplars were being lashed this way and that by the wind.

"I don't think this is such a good idea," said the girl. "The story has been happy so far, but I don't know if it's going to be the same today."

"Hanumaan! Hanumaan!" they shouted above the howling winds.

Hanumaan appeared from the bushes and called them over. They followed him through the gap in the laurel leaves and found themselves in a sheltered cave made from leaves. Once inside it, they felt safe again, protected from the wind and from its howling.

"I bet today's the day when Raavana, Lord of the Dark Force, enters the story," said the boy. "Your father, the Lord of the Wind, seems ready for a fight."

"Wait and listen to what happens next," said Hanumaan and the story continued...

RAAMA AND HIS BROTHERS, their wives and parents, having celebrated the marriages for two whole weeks, felt that it was time to return to Ayodhya. They said their farewells to Seeta's father, the good King Janaka, wished prosperity, peace and health upon his kingdom, and set off on the journey home, laden with thousands of presents and followed by hundreds of servants and an army of helpers.

The royal messengers sped ahead and, by the time the

family reached Ayodhya, the roads were covered with perfumes and the petals of a million flowers. People lined the streets to clap and cheer their brave young princes and their wives. Servants rushed from the palace with beautiful silk shawls for the queens and the new princesses, and robes for the King and his four brave sons.

In this happy city the princes lived for many years, growing stronger and wiser. They delighted all with their skill in the tournaments. They were to be seen in the market square listening to the stories of the old men and visiting monks. Their wives, too, soon won the hearts of the people with their gentle ways. And gentlest of all was Seeta, that rose among ladies, with a voice that put the nightingale to shame, with a touch that made the roughest minds calm. Wherever she walked, peace followed.

Then, one day the King made an announcement: *"I have consulted all who are wise and all who know about the art of ruling kingdoms. They have given their blessing to my decision that Raama is to be crowned king."*

You can imagine the celebration that followed that announcement. Everyone in the city was wild with excitement because everyone loved Raama as their own son. They loved his bravery, his sweet words, his gentle nature, the way he protected his wife, the way he never spoke a lie. They loved his eyes and hair and skill in warfare and knowledge of the ancient wisdom. There was not one good person who wasn't pleased with the news.

BUT DEEP in the dark corridors of the palace there was one black heart — the hunchback maidservant of the second queen was full of anger when she heard the news. As quickly as her twisted legs could carry her, she hobbled through the corridors of the palace, burst into her mistress's room and woke her from her sleep.

"*Where is your son Bharata?*" growled the maid.

"*Why? What is it?*" asked the queen, rubbing the dream from her eyes.

"*Where is Bharata? Have you not heard the news?*" said the hunchback.

The astonished queen said: "*He's visiting his grandfather with Lakshmana's twin brother. What's the news?*"

The hunchback grabbed the queen by the arm and pulled her over to the window. Down below, the city was in full preparation for the celebration. There were acrobats and musicians, flags and garlands, shopkeepers giving gifts to strangers, children with sugar candy and large mugs of sweet juice, silk and bright colours, laughter and singing — all happy for Raama's big day.

"*It must be good news,*" said the queen, quite delighted with the sights. "*Let's go and join them.*"

The maid pushed her back onto the bed. "*Silly, silly, child. This is a black day, the day that means the death of your son. Cry. Scream. Tear your hair out. This is a black, black day.*"

"*What's up, woman?*" said the queen, quite disturbed now.

"*The king has announced that Raama is to be crowned tomorrow,*" said the hunchback.

THE QUEEN became wild with happiness like the people in the streets below and, in her delight, forgot she was a queen, jumped up and down on her bed with joy and ran

around the room like a girl again. But she was grabbed by the hunchback and pushed back onto the bed. *"Stop it!"* hissed the evil woman. *"Stop and think! Why does the King wait till your son Bharata is away before he makes this announcement? What is the trick up his sleeve? When Raama hears the news, will he not become crazed with power and fear all he believes to be his enemies? And who is next in line after Raama to be king?"*

The words entered the queen's ears like poison and the maid, seeing this, continued: *"Good . . . you're starting to think again . . . Bharata is next in line to be king . . . And Raama knows it and will not be happy till Bharata is out of the way."*

"That's not like Raama," sobbed the queen. *"Why are you saying these things?"*

"I'm only saying it, my precious, because I love you and want what's best for you and your son." Then the hunchback maid continued to speak more poisonous words till the queen slowly became full of poison herself.

"What's to be done?" asked the queen.

The maid grinned an evil grin. *"Remember,"* she said, *"many years ago when the King was wounded in battle and all the men around him had been killed ... wasn't it you who saved him and brought him back to life? And what did he promise you ... ?"*

"Two boons," said the queen, sobbing.

"And what did you say at that time?"

"Not now, I said, I'll ask for the boons later," said the queen.

"The day has come for you to ask for the boons," said the maid.

The queen's heart had turned to ice by now. *"You're right,"* she said. *"The King owes me two boons."*

The maid rubbed her bony hands together. *"Shall we ask that the first one is that he puts your son Bharata on the throne instead of Raama?"*

"We shall," said the queen.

"And shall we ask that he banishes Raama into the forest for fourteen years as the second boon?" whispered the hunchback.

"We shall," hissed the queen. And that is what she did.

"NO!" screamed the girl. "Why is this happening, Hanumaan? It's been a happy story till now and you've gone and made it all horrible."

Hanumaan didn't look up at the children. He pretended he was busy examining some leaves, head bowed. "It's the way life sometimes unfolds," he mumbled. Then he sat up and looked the children straight in the eyes and said: "Is it all happiness and sunlight in your lives? Or, sometimes, doesn't disaster strike?"

"Obviously," said the girl. "But we are not like Raama. He's good, isn't he?"

"That he most certainly is," said Hanumaan. "But in Ayodhya everyone believed that disaster doesn't come from this life and that each of us are born over and over again to complete unfinished business. And sometimes the bad actions of the past return to give us the hard knocks in the present."

"What did Raama do that was so bad?" said the boy.

"It wasn't Raama who had sinned. It was his father, the King," said Hanumaan. "In his past, the King was quite proud of his skill as an archer. So to show off one day, he covered his eyes with a blindfold and went hunting. His ears played tricks on him and he ended up killing a young boy who was fetching water for his blind parents. When the parents heard that their son had been killed by this proud king, they cursed him with these words: 'Just when your son is about to fill your heart with joy, may that happiness be stolen from you.' This was the curse that went into action on the day the king was happiest — the day he was to put Raama on the throne."

"How did Raama take it?" asked the girl.

"Listen," said Hanumaan . . .

WHEN THE KING heard his second wife ask for the two terrible boons he fell to the floor in shock. He begged her to ask for something else.

"Do you want new clothes of fine silk, embroidered in real gold?" said the King.

The queen said: *"No."*

"What about fine new jewellery, rubies from the North and white metal from the heavens?"

The queen said: *"No."*

"Ah, I know what you'll like," said the King, *"a splendid*

new palace in the hills, made of the purest white marble, with two hundred servants and fifty elephants of your own."

The queen shook her head.

"Please ask me for anything, but not what you've asked for," begged the King.

But the queen, her heart now as cold as ice, shook her head. *"For my first boon, I want my son Bharata to have the throne,"* she repeated. *"And for my second, I want Raama banished into the forest for fourteen years."*

"No!" shouted the King. *"Anything but that!"*

But the queen folded her arms and shook her head. *"Go and fetch Raama,"* she snapped to one of the guards. *"I want him to hear of his future from his own father's lips."* An evil smile spread across her face.

The King threw himself at her feet. *"Please, please change your mind. How has Raama ever hurt you? Spare him, please,"* begged the King.

His wife shook her head. The King fainted in grief.

People rushed to the King and carried him onto the couch. Some muttered: *"Shame! Shame!"* But this did not disturb the queen. She stood alone in one half of the room with only the hunchback maid beside her.

The wise Counsellor said: *"Can you not see the hurt you have caused?"*

The queen just turned away and said: *"Where are those people I sent off to fetch Raama?"*

Footsteps were heard running down the corridor. The door to the room opened and Raama saw his father lying as if dead.

At that moment the wind howled like fury in the trees in the park and a great branch crashed down on the leaf cave where the children sat listening to Hanumaan's story.

Hanumaan snatched them, one under each of his powerful arms and ran and leapt to the edge of the park. "Run home, run!" he shouted. "Come back tomorrow when the anger of the wind has calmed."

The children ran . . . They reached home puffing, frightened at the fury of the storm. Aunt Sissey was angry too. She sent them both upstairs to change out of their wet things.

"Aunt Sissey has a heart like ice," said the boy.

"She has a temper like fire, though," said the girl. She tossed the boy a towel to dry his hair. "What would you do if all that had happened to you, and you were about to be banished?" she asked.

The boy gave a little leap, spread his feet apart, clenched his jaw, raised his fists and gave a fierce frown. "I'd fight for my crown . . ."

"Yes, but what would you do if you were Raama?" said the girl.

A calmness came over the boy. His face became quiet and fine. His eyes fell to the ground. "I guess I'd just know what to do."

The girl gave him a big hug. He pushed her away: "Stop being so soppy. You know I hate it. I bet Seeta never did stuff like that to Raama."

"I bet she did," said the girl.

Banished to the forest

THE NEXT DAY was a day of rain. It was rain such as the children had never seen before because the air was totally still and yet the rain just poured and poured. Everything in the garden had a drowned look — the bushes and flowers and trees were not stirred by the wind, but just stayed where they were and let the rain pour down on their bowed heads.

"I'm sure the Lord of the Wind is crying," said the girl.

"That's put an end to today's story, I guess," said the boy.

"The sky is crying because the cold-hearted queen wants Raama banished," said the girl.

"We're banished too," said the boy, "stuck here at home when we want to be in Hanumaan's world."

"I feel like standing here and crying," said the girl. The boy looked at her and found himself saying: "There's no need for that."

Immediately the girl stopped her sadness. "Your voice ...," she said. "It sounded exactly like Hanumaan's."

The sound of Hanumaan's voice continued ...

WHEN RAAMA SAW his father lying as if dead, he immediately rushed over to him and took his head in his lap. He looked around at the others. *"Will someone tell me what's happened,"* he pleaded.

Bharata's mother, the second queen, turned her eyes away from Raama and said: *"Your father has something he wants to tell you. It is about your future."*

The King started to stir in Raama's lap. When he saw his son's face, tears filled his eyes, but Raama remained steady. *"I have been tricked,"* cried the King. *"She made me do it."*

"Do what?" asked Raama. There was the sound of angry voices at the door and Lakshmana pushed his way into the room, followed by Seeta.

"What's going on here?" demanded Lakshmana.

"I have been tricked into promising that Bharata will have the throne instead of Raama," cried the King.

"The answer is simple," said Lakshmana. *"I won't let it happen. For one moment I thought that there was a bigger problem."*

"I have also been tricked into banishing Raama into the forest for fourteen years," said the King.

"Who did this wicked thing?" shouted Lakshmana.

The King pointed to the queen who was standing in the shadows at the far end of the room. *"Let me kill her,"* screamed Lakshmana. *"And let me kill Bharata."*

Raama took hold of his brother's arm and made him say sorry for speaking so harshly to the queen. *"There is to be no talk of killing,"* he said. Then turning to the King he asked if he had given his word. The King nodded.

Raama hung his head for a moment. Tears from Seeta's eyes fell to the cold marble floor of the room. Lakshmana was puffing with anger like a mad bull about to charge. Raama saw all this and then a wonderful thing happened — he smiled!

"It really is a simple matter," he said. *"A king's word is his bond. Let the promises stand. Bharata will make a very good king — kind, loving and just. As for me, fourteen years in the forest will be an adventure."*

"In that case," said Lakshmana, *"I want to come with you."*

Then Seeta added: *"There is no way that I will be without my lord. I will walk in the forest bare-foot in front of him so that my feet pick up the thorns from his path. I will sit with him in the evenings and we will talk till the birds sing us to sleep. In the mornings we will wash in sparkling streams and feed off fresh fruit. I most certainly will not be left behind."*

There was nothing that Raama could say that would make her change her mind.

EARLY NEXT MORNING the three of them got ready to leave the sleeping city. Raama went to his mother first and touched her feet. *"Take care of father,"* he said. With tears streaming down her cheeks, she laid her hand on Raama's gentle head and gave him her blessing.

Next Raama went to the second queen — Bharata's mother, the one who had caused all the trouble — and, bowing before her, said: *"If I have hurt you in any way, please forgive me. Take care of my brother Bharata and allow him to rule wisely."*

He found Lakshmana with his mother, the third queen. She looked up at Raama, eyes red with crying, and she hugged Lakshmana and kissed him on his forehead.

Raama, Seeta and Lakshmana were ready to leave.

"Wait," cried a voice from the shadows. It was the hunchbacked maid. *"Banishment to the forest means living like the forest people. Take off all those fine clothes and jewels."* She tossed a bundle of rags at their feet. *"These will be your clothes for the next fourteen years,"* she laughed.

Raama once more pleaded with Seeta to change her mind. Seeta shook her head and went to change out of her beautiful clothes. And, although she returned dressed in bark-cloth, and her hair matted with mud, and rough wooden sandals

covered her feet, her beauty shone like the brilliance of a
million stars. She led the way to the chariot that was to carry
them to the forest.

When the ladies of the palace realised that this was not a
horrible dream, they began crying and wailing and all
through the palace was heard their sorrow, like the sound of
geese in pain. The homes in the city that had been filled
with the sound of music and laughter the night before were
now filled with crying and shrieking. People ran after the
chariot, trying to stop it. Even the heavens, trying to stop it,
shook off stars that crashed down onto the road in mighty
explosions that shattered the windows.

Then as night fell, the chariot slowed down as it passed through the last villages in the kingdom.

The streets were empty. Tiny oil lamps flickered in the houses. In the silence of the night Raama heard the crying of women, and men speaking angrily about the wicked deed of the queen and about the shame and sorrow of the King. Seeta put her hands to her ears because she did not want to hear any more.

"Take us to the furthest edge of the kingdom," said Raama to the charioteer. *"I know even this place too well and it reminds me of my father who is sick with sadness."*

BACK IN THE PALACE the King had cried so much and cursed his second wife so often that he became pale and weak. He called Raama's mother to his room and together they spent the whole night talking of happy times and mourning the cruel thing that had happened.

Then, finally, the King cried out: *"It is my stupid sin that has brought this pain upon us. I am cursed!"* He fell once more to the floor — dead.

The ministers rushed to the palace. *"The city is without a king,"* they said. *"This makes us weak — our enemies can take us over. We need a king."* Someone wanted to get Raama back, but the wise Counsellor reminded them of the King's promise to his second wife that Bharata would have the throne. But Bharata was still away in his grandfather's home with his youngest brother.

Messengers were quickly sent to bring Bharata back. They were to tell him nothing of what had happened, but only to say: *"You are needed home immediately."*

When Bharata and his brother got the news they became excited. *"The time must have arrived for Raama to be crowned,"* said Bharata. Finding themselves the fastest chariot, they returned home with all speed.

Imagine the princes' surprise when, instead of seeing decorations and fireworks and crowds playing music, they saw a city of tears with empty streets and black drapes across the windows.

Bharata charged up the palace steps to his mother's room. *"What's going on?"* he asked, puffing out of breath.

The second queen was well pleased to see her son and said: *"We must hurry and prepare for the coronation."*

"But where are all the acrobats and flags and music?" said Bharata. *"If Raama is to be crowned king, then why is everyone looking so sad?"*

The queen threw her arms wide open and with a big smile on her face she cried. *"Surprise! YOU are to be made king, not Raama."*

"Don't play games with me now, mother," said Bharata. *"Where's Raama?"*

The queen flung open her arms again and cried: *"Thrown out of the city! The crown is yours, the kingdom is yours. You are the next king."*

Bharata became annoyed, thinking his mother was still playing silly games. *"We'll see about this,"* he said. *"Father will tell me the truth."* He ran down the corridor, passing servants who were crying, soldiers who were weeping, and priests saying prayers for the dead. When he burst into his father's room and saw the dead king covered in a white sheet, he fell to his knees. *"What's happening?"* he shouted. *"Will somebody tell me where Raama is?"*

Then he heard the full, horrible story.

"MOTHER!" he boomed.

The queen entered the room with bowed head.

"Why did you do this? You silly, silly woman!" shouted Bharata when he saw his mother.

"I did it for you, my son," she replied and tried to get him to smile.

"Do not touch me!" he cried.

Tears trickled down his mother's cheek for the first time since her dreadful deed as she slowly realised what she had done.

Bharata shook his head and said: *"Do you really think that I would be king while Raama is still alive somewhere in the dangerous forest? And what about Seeta, that pure princess who has known only the comforts of the palace and has slept only on the softest mattresses? How can you have done this?"*

The queen tried to take his hand, but he pushed her off and she fell to the floor. Nobody moved to help her except the horrible hunchback maid.

Bharata's younger brother rushed over to the old hag, grabbed her by the hair and drew his sword. *"It's all your evil doing!"* he screamed and raised the sword to cut her head off.

"Stop!" shouted Bharata. *"What would Raama say if he heard that you had killed a woman — even though she deserves to die? Would Raama do such a thing?"*

His brother shook his head.

"Stay here and protect the queens," Bharata said to him. *"Raama belongs in this city and on the throne."* He sent for a chariot with fresh horses. *"I'm going to bring him back now,"* he said and stormed out of the room.

Watching the whole scene was the royal Counsellor. He

smiled and nodded, *"Bharata has all the makings of a wise king. His actions today give me great comfort."*

Bharata's mother sniffed and looked up at him. *"So I didn't do such a bad thing after all, did I?"* she said.

Without even glancing at her, the Counsellor walked out of the room.

"I can't believe that Bharata's mother can be so cruel," said the girl.

"She's evil," said the boy. "Why else would she do such a thing?"

"I wonder if our mother would love us so much that she would hurt all sorts of people just so that we got the best," said the girl.

"She isn't that sort of person," said the boy.

"Surely it was the same with Bharata's mother. How did she end up becoming so wicked?"

"I don't know," said the boy. "But I do know one thing about our mother — she always says that she expects us to stand on our own two feet." He flopped back on his bed, shut his eyes and was soon asleep.

The girl looked down at his peaceful face. Then she remembered that Hanumaan had never appeared to tell them the story, but that his voice had spoken through the boy. "No wonder he's tired out," she smiled.

Day 7
The good brother

AFTER THEY HAD FINISHED their jobs around the house the next day, the children returned to their bedroom. Hardly one word had been spoken during the day. Each time Aunt Sissey said, "Do this", they just got on with the job without a word.

When they were finally alone the girl said to the boy: "I hope you realise that it was you who told yesterday's story. Who needs Hanumaan with you around?"

"I need him," said the boy. He turned his head to face the ceiling and called: "Hanumaan where are you?"

"Here," said Hanumaan's voice. The children spun round in surprise. There in the middle of the room was Hanumaan.

"Where did you come from?" said the girl. "How did you get here?"

"You called," he said with a smile. "Shall the story continue now?"

"Yes please."

Hanumaan began to speak...

ONCE BHARATA DISCOVERED what had happened, he was determined to get Raama back to the city. He ordered the fastest chariot to stand waiting for him at the palace gates. But when he got there he found that the whole city had gathered, including Raama's mother, the first queen.

"I have now lost both my son and my husband," she wept. *"Life in the palace has no more happiness for me. I will join Raama and Seeta and Lakshmana in the forest."*

Nothing that Bharata said would make her change her mind.

So the vast army slowly made their way through the sad

city. Some people rode on donkeys, some on carts pulled by huge bulls, a few of them rode on camels and elephants. There were thousands and thousands of them — young and old, women and men, grandfathers and children. The other queens also wanted to come and so did their servants — all wanted their Raama back.

The shops in the city were left boarded up and empty, the cows had stopped giving milk, the birds had stopped singing. Even the royal peacocks had shed their beautiful feathers and roamed around like ugly things.

Soon the walls of the city were left far behind. The army followed the road that Raama had taken. By the banks of the dark river they saw the grass bed where Raama and Seeta had spent their first night of exile, and the crying became even louder.

Raama's mother said that it was a crime for the beautiful Seeta to sleep like an animal in a bed of straw with no one there to brush her hair or lay out fresh clothes for her.

Bharata gently led the queen away and told her not to make herself too sad. *"In a couple of days, you'll see Raama in the flesh and we'll take him back with us,"* he said.

THE CITIZENS of Ayodhya crossed the river and entered a beautiful part of the country in which many monks and wise men lived. Bharata told everyone to stop and he went ahead alone on foot to the hermitage of a very powerful sage.

The sage greeted Bharata, offered him water to drink and to wash the dust of the journey from his feet. Then he asked for news from Ayodhya. Bharata told him of all that had happened and said: *"I will not become king, not while Raama is still alive. I am going to bring him back."*

"You are a good brother," said the sage. *"Rest here for the night."* But, looking around, he asked Bharata why he had come alone on foot. Where were the queens? Where was the vast army that left the city?

Bharata explained that the army was so huge, with one hundred elephants, one thousand chariots and ten thousand people, that he did not want them trampling all over the beautiful hermitage.

"Nonsense," said the sage. *"Bring them here. I will make preparations to receive them."* He shut his eyes and became perfectly still and everything began to change.

By the time Bharata returned with his followers, the whole place had been transformed. White houses had been built for the men, golden tents for the queens. Servant girls dressed in heavenly white clothes poured drink into golden goblets for the soldiers from lakes full of wine. Huge platters of the most delicious food hung in the trees and music played everywhere.

The crowd ate and drank and swam in warm waters under a sky filled to glory with stars. Thus the celebrations carried on deep into the night till one by one the men, women, children, soldiers and sages fell asleep. And silence covered the camp.

People had enjoyed the entertainment so much that some of them thought that this was heaven and they didn't want to go back home or to go forward into the forest.

But all through the celebrations, Bharata had only one name on his mind: Raama. Raama. Raama. So when morning came Bharata woke with the name Raama on his mind. He thanked the sage for his wonderful entertainment, but said that he wanted to go on to find Raama.

"Good," said the sage. *"The entertainment I put on was a test*

*to see how strong was your wish to find Raama. Your words
today have proved that your search is true. Whether you succeed or
fail is not important. What's important is that you have chosen
the right action."*

He placed his hand on Bharata's head and gave him his
blessing, adding: *"Do not judge your mother, the queen, too
harshly. Raama's exile will result in great good for the gods in
heaven and good for people on earth. Remember that."*

THE VAST ARMY followed Bharata into the blue
mountains full of wild deer and antelopes and flocks of white
birds. *"Search the hillside for Raama's camp,"* ordered Bharata
and scouts set off to the east and west, north and south.

After a while the scouts who had gone north returned with
the good news that they had spotted a leaf-hut, probably the
camp of Raama.

They were right, but they weren't the only ones on
lookout. Lakshmana, hearing the noise made by the army of
people, had climbed a high tree to see what was happening.

"Bharata is on his way here with a huge army," he shouted
to Raama. *"That wicked brother! Not satisfied that you have
been exiled, he wants to kill you to make sure that the kingdom is
his till he dies. Hurry Raama, let's hide in the trees and kill them
all before they harm us."*

But Raama would hear none of this. *"Gather fruit and
fresh water. Seeta, prepare garlands of the brightest flowers for
the queens. Prepare beds of sweet smelling grasses for the tired
army,"* he said.

And by the time Bharata arrived at the camp, he was faced
with Raama sitting proudly at the entrance to his hut, Seeta

sitting beside him and Lakshmana standing guard. Tears immediately filled Bharata's eyes and he dropped to his knees, beating the ground with his fists. *"Raama, Raama, why has this terrible thing happened. I promise I knew nothing about the evil deeds of my mother — I don't have the slightest wish to be king. Please forget everything and return with me to the palace and take your rightful place."*

Raama turned to Lakshmana and said: *"See, I told you. Bharata is a good brother. But I cannot return to the city because I have given my promise to our father that I would follow his command. That's what I am going to do."*

At that moment Raama's mother pushed her way through the crowd and threw her arms around her son's neck. *"You haven't heard the news,"* she cried. *"Your father died of a broken heart soon after you left. Now you are free to return. If not for your sake, then for Seeta's and for my sake, return."*

Raama looked down at his sorrowing mother and felt on the point of being overcome with emotion. *"Mother, you have raised me to be noble, truthful and honourable. How can I forget all that for just one kingdom. You were there when, in front of all assembled, my father said: 'Go to the forest for fourteen years, Bharata is to be made king.' That was the word of the King, that is the law! I agreed to stand by it then and will follow it now."*

Then, putting an arm around Bharata's shoulders, Raama walked with his good brother alone and told him all about the duties of a king. He reminded him that he should rule wisely and for the good of all. They talked for many hours and Bharata had become steady by the time they returned. He looked like a king!

"Raama has spoken the law," he said to the assembled army. *"His wisdom makes me full of shame for my unsteady mind.*

Today we shall return to the city. The kingdom will have a king."

Then, kneeling, he gently removed Raama's sandals. *"These sandals of Raama will be placed on the throne to show all who visit us who the real king is. As for me, I will live in a simple house in a nearby village and rule in my brother's name."* His heart was full of sadness, but his voice remained steady.

Turning to Raama, he said: *"If you do not return after fourteen years, I will build a huge fire and throw myself into it."* Holding Raama's wooden sandals over his head, Bharata shouted: *"Long live King Raama!"* And the crowd cheered.

The queens who were choked with tears were unable to say goodbye. Raama touched each one on the head — his mother first, then Lakshmana's and finally the mother of Bharata who had caused this horrible sadness. He turned and entered his own hut.

Hanumaan stopped his story because the little girl had thrown herself face down on the bed and was crying. He placed a gentle hand on her back. "In this drama of life, everything that appears will also pass. So let the sadness pass. Raama did. Seeta did."

He cleared his throat, sat upright and said: "Tomorrow, the story will change scene. Raama found that wherever he looked the beautiful hills reminded him of the goodness of Bharata and made him sad. So he decided to leave the place behind and enter the dark forest beyond the hills. When you enter the place where the Dark Force roams, when there are wild beasts and demons all around, it is not useful to be crying all the time — your heart needs to be steady, your mind needs to be alert, your weapons need to be sharp. So look out . . . we are about to enter the dark forest."

Hanumaan stood on the window ledge and leapt onto the branches of the apple tree in the garden. The girl watched the tiny tree bend and creak under his weight, showering leaves and fruit all over the grass. Then it stopped. Hanumaan had gone and so had the trembling in her heart.

Day 8
Adventures in the forest

THE CHILDREN managed to get Aunt Sissey to picnic in the park the next day. The stormy weather of the few previous days was behind them and, although the sun was not out in its full glory, the weather report had promised a sunny afternoon.

It didn't take them long to leave Aunt Sissey, with her nose stuck in a magazine about the lives of the rich and famous, and escape to the secret trees.

It was like the first day they met Hanumaan. The Lord of the Wind rattled the trees, the carpet was on the grass with fruit and nuts and Hanumaan was at the top of the highest poplar.

"Is this the bit of the story where Raama meets you?" the girl asked Hanumaan.

"Not yet," said the monkey. "Be patient. The Dark Force has yet to make its move. It won't be long. Be patient and listen . . ."

RAAMA, SEETA AND LAKSHMANA left the beautiful blue hills and entered the edge of the Dandaka forest. Wolves howled and black ravens filled the trees. Seeta kept close to the two princes — Lakshmana leading and Raama following at the back, both like hunters, ready to spring into action at the first sign of danger.

They didn't have to wait long. A most horrible creature, the size of a mountain, leapt into the path and looked down at the three tiny people. His eyes were black and bulging and his mouth hung open showing rotten teeth in which were stuck the bones of a tiger he had just eaten. On his spear hung the bodies of three lions, four tigers, two leopards,

four baby deer and the head of an enormous elephant.

The two princes stood their ground in front of the mighty demon. With one blow the demon knocked them both rolling into the trees and grabbed Seeta and tucked her into his belt. She screamed and struggled and called to Raama for help.

Raama untangled himself from the bushes and sent three arrows speeding towards the demon's heart. They entered his chest with a hiss like angry snakes. But nothing happened — he didn't fall to the ground. He plucked the arrows from his chest and crumpled them in his hairy fist as if they were made of straw.

"I am the demon that can't be killed with weapons!" he roared.

Lakshmana's spear whistled through the air and struck the creature in the neck. Blood started to pour and the monster screamed in anger and dashed the spear to the ground. He spun round to face the two princes. His black feet kicked up forest dust, his powerful fists smashed down trees in his way. Seeta managed to struggle free and dropped to the ground just at the moment the monster roared in fury and rushed at the princes.

He knocked them unconscious, lifted them onto his shoulders and bound off towards his cave. Seeta ran after the creature, hurling stones at it, hitting it with branches. *"Spare them!"* she cried. *"Take me instead."*

The courage and fight in Seeta's voice revived Raama. With the fury of a thunderbolt, he slammed both fists down onto the monster's arms and heard the bone snap. Lakshmana did the same. The monster fell to the forest floor with a thud. He lay there without moving but they could see that he was not dead.

"Quickly! Dig a pit large enough to trap an elephant," said Raama. *"We must bury him before he wakes. Our weapons are of no use here. Seeta, call out if he so much as moves an eyelash."* Raama and Laskshmana threw themselves into the job of digging with a fury of wild boars.

"Hurry!" cried Seeta. *"I think I saw him move."*

Raama rushed over to the demon and stood with one foot on his neck while his brother and Seeta carried on digging. *"Dig! Dig faster! We must bury him in the pit,"* shouted Raama.

Suddenly the monster stopped struggling. In a gentle voice he addressed Raama: *"O lion among heroes,"* he said. *"In my rage I did not recognise you as the mighty prince of Ayodhya. But the words you have just spoken have brought me to my senses. I too used to be a prince but a curse turned me into this terrible creature. My only freedom would come when I was killed by the mighty prince Raama who would break my arms and bury me in a pit.*"

Raama removed his foot from the monster's throat.

"*I am dying, lord,*" said the creature. "*But I wish to repay you for lifting my curse. Take the northern path from here and you will find forest dwellers who need your help.*" With that the monster died.

Raama and Lakshmana rolled his body into the pit and, as they threw the first shovel-full of mud onto his hairy body, they saw it change back into the form of a handsome young prince.

THEY FOLLOWED the northern path through the forest as the cursed creature had told them to and came across the hermitages of many monks and sages. At each stop Raama would be blessed. One sage whose simple home was showered in golden light from heaven greeted Raama. "*My prayers and good works have won me a place in the the third level of heaven,*" said the old man. "*Please accept this place as a gift.*"

Raama smiled and stood before the sage. "*Thank you, good sir, but Raama has no need to take from you your hard-earned place in heaven,*" he said. Then his body began to glow with the brilliance of a thousand suns — so bright that Seeta and Lakshmana fell to the ground and covered their eyes. The sage became exceedingly happy and his eyes sparkled with pure bliss at the sight of Raama's shining form.

When word of this meeting spread through the forest, hundreds of hermits flocked to Raama and asked for his protection. They showed him the remains of dead friends who had been killed by the Night Rangers.

"Fear not," said Raama. *"I will make this forest safe again. I will show no mercy to the Dark Force."*

THAT NIGHT as the others slept under the blanket of a peaceful night sky, Seeta whispered to Raama: *"There is something that I find very worrying and I don't know how to tell you."*

Raama smiled at her and said: *"Simply open your heart and speak."*

Seeta said: *"The wise say that three evils follow men. The first is to speak lies — and I know that you are totally free from that one. The second is to want to take another man's wife — there too you are fully blameless. But there is the third evil which I am worried might catch you if you are not careful and that is to cause hurt without good reason. When I hear you say that you will kill the Night Rangers without mercy it worries me."*

Hearing his wife's words made Raama pleased. *"You couldn't have spoken those words unless there was love in your heart. But I was born into the race of warriors and it is my duty to protect all those who are weak. Even if I had not given my promise to these forest dwellers, it would still be my duty to protect them. Your speech has now made you dearer to me than life itself."*

Seeta snuggled into Raama's arms and fell asleep with a smile on her face.

THE WEEKS AND MONTHS that passed were busy for Raama and Lakshmana. They were like fire in the forest — sparking here, flashing there, their arrows and darts lighting up the night sky, weakening the power of the Dark Force as demon after demon hit the forest floor.

The Dandaka forest slowly resumed its natural beauty. Tame deer roamed the place again and animals of every kind returned. The sunlit skies were full of the songs of every type of bird and beast of the day, and the darkness was full of the croaks and hisses and roars of the beasts of night. But everyone was safe.

Raama, Seeta and Lakshmana moved deeper into the forest until they came to a high mountain which was kissed by the clouds and warmed by the sun's rays. Lakshmana, who by now had become a great house-builder, soon made the three of them wonderful huts from leaves and mud. He created all sorts of handy things for the home: bowls and shelves, tables and hammocks, plates and chairs, benches, spoons, swings, fans, water pots, oil lamps, ladders, bridges, carts — all out of wood and stones, vines and leaves.

Each morning Raama and Seeta would bathe in pools covered by perfumed lotus blossoms, each night they would pray under the canopy of the stars. Animals of every sort started to appear — tiny dappled deer were the first. Seeta held out some grain in her palm and the gentle creatures looking this way and that, ears and nose twitching, took one step closer and then another, till they let her stroke their necks. All creatures loved Seeta. Even tigers allowed her to tickle their bellies.

THERE WAS ONE creature who became a special friend. This was a massive vulture called Jataayu.

When Lakshmana first saw Jataayu soaring high among

the clouds, he felt certain that it was a Night Ranger preparing to swoop down on them. He had his bow in hand, ready to let fly a deadly arrow, when Raama stopped him.

"Look how steady he is," said Raama. *"If he was from the Dark Force he would be quivering with fear by now."*

The two brothers watched the mighty bird glide gracefully on the high winds and then suddenly he bent back his wings and plumetted towards the earth. Then, just as they thought he would surely crash, the vulture's dive flattened out and he circled slowly once, twice, three times above the princes and floated to the forest floor.

"Salutations, Prince Raama," said the bird. *"Greetings, Prince Lakshmana. I am Jataayu, king of vultures, here to watch over you. I was once a good friend to your father."*

Soon Jataayu became a close companion to Seeta. He told her the stories of how all creatures began. First about the owls and vultures, hawks, swans, flamingo and water-fowl. Then the deer, bears, buffaloes and yaks. He told her next about powerful lions and monkeys, lovers of the forest, together with tigers, elephants, cows, horses, hooded serpents and slithering snakes.

Seeta loved the stories of this first of vultures and Jataayu had a special fondness for Seeta. He said to Raama: *"I will take up abode in this part of the forest so that I can keep watch over Seeta when you are away with Lakshmana."*

Raama was filled with delight. He felt that Seeta was now well-protected. Little did he know how much the brave and fierce vulture would soon have to do to keep his promise to guard Seeta . . .

Suddenly there was a crashing through the bushes. The children shot to their feet. Hanumaan leapt to the top of the poplar with one bound.

Aunt Sissey stumbled into the magic circle of grass, her hair all over her face, her shawl half off her shoulders.

"So this is what you get up to," she said, grinning.

"This is our secret grove," shouted the boy. "You have no right to be here."

"I was just curious to know what you got up to," said Aunt Sissey, still smiling, trying to push the wild strands of hair back into a bun.

"Well, now you know," said the girl. "You gave us such a fright crashing in like that."

Aunt Sissey patted her cheek. "I don't want to frighten you, my dear," she said, eyes bulging, "but when you keep disappearing like little spies, leaving me all alone in the park, what do you expect me to do? Just sit there?"

"What's wrong with your silly magazines?" snapped the boy.

"I don't know if I like the tone of your voice, young man," said Aunt Sissey, no longer smiling. She snatched up the rug. "And where did this come from? My attic? And who gave you permission to take it?"

"It's not yours! Leave us alone," yelled the boy. The girl tried to calm him down, but Aunt Sissey pulled her away by the arm, "You're coming home with me this instant!"

"NO!" yelled the boy. An orange flew through the air. He watched with horror as his weapon arched surely towards its target in slow motion . . . till . . . BANG! Aunt Sissey had a bleeding nose.

"That's it!" she yelled. "I've had enough!"

Locked in their bedroom that evening the children listened through the door. They could make out snatches of the telephone conversation between Aunt Sissey and their parents. Whatever else she said, there was one thing the children were certain about: the holiday with Aunt Sissey had come to an end.

Day 9
The she-demon

THE DAWN HAD JUST BROKEN the next morning when something the size of an orange burst in through the bedroom window, shattering the glass. It landed on the dressing table and came to rest on the tiny hand mirror that belonged to the girl.

The children, still half asleep, couldn't work out what was happening. But then they heard a familiar voice calling them from the dressing table.

"Hanumaan!" they exclaimed with one voice.

It was Hanumaan, shrunk right down in size, sitting cross-legged on a lace doily. Their jaws fell open with amazement. He put one long black finger to his lips and said: "No time to answer your questions, now. It's time to carry on the story."

"But you're so small," said the boy.

"It's a trick I've found very useful when trouble looms . . . but that comes later in the story. So stop talking and just listen . . ." Hanumaan shut his eyes and sat very still for a moment. Then he started to speak . . .

RAAMA, SEETA AND LAKSHMANA lived happily for thirteen years in the beautiful forest among the holy men and the friendly animals and birds. It seemed as if nothing would spoil their happiness. Sadly, this was not to be the case. Trouble was just around the corner.

It happened like this . . .

One evening, after they had had their bath and eaten a beautiful meal and said their prayers, the three of them sat under the dusk red sky, cooled by a gentle breeze that blew across the lake, talking about how wonderful life in exile had turned out to be.

Under the evening sky, the whole forest was pulsing with life. A flock of geese flew across the large red ball of the sun, honking as they passed over. The tops of the trees were aflame with huge red flowers, dripping with fragrance and nectar. A family of monkeys swung through them, chattering and squawking their monkey talk. The sound of crickets filled the air and, every so often, there was a deep throated roar of tigers that had come out for the night.

"How I will miss all this," sighed Seeta. She slipped her hand into Raama's and he knew that he loved his Seeta very, very much.

SUDDENLY there was a different sound in the forest. Tiny animals scattered in all directions, birds left the trees in swarms like black waves, wolves began to howl. Someone, something was approaching . . . and heading straight for the camp. Raama put his arm around Seeta's shoulders. Lakshmana rushed off for his bow and arrows.

It turned out to be a very beautiful woman — at least it looked like one. In fact, this was one of the most ugly and fierce demons of the forest, none other than the sister of Raavana, Lord of the Dark Force. She had been hiding in the trees, spying on Raama and Seeta and had soon fallen under the spell of Raama. *"I want that man for myself,"* she thought. So, using her magic powers she changed her form from that of an ugly hag with purple skin and great big boils on her face to a beautiful, slender maid.

She approached Raama and, ignoring Seeta beside him, said: *"You may be dressed in the bark clothes and antelope skins of a hermit, but you stand as tall and proud as a prince. Leave this place and come with me. Together we can explore all the magic secrets of this forest that no human has ever seen before. I will show you the river that flows uphill, the white trees that grow in underground caves, the lion with two heads and the elephant tribe that have golden tusks."*

"*But I already have a wife,*" said Raama gently. "*I can't just leave her and go off with you.*"

"*What? You mean that thing?*" said the she-demon, poking Seeta with a long pointed finger. "*She's skinny and weak. Me, on the other hand, I can bite off the head of a wolf with my bare teeth.*"

"*I don't know if I like the sound of that,*" said Raama.

The she-demon continued to try to win him over and continued to push and poke Seeta till Raama no longer thought it was funny.

Finally, in an attempt to get rid of her, he pointed to Lakshmana who stood leaning against his long bow, watching the scene and laughing at the whole show. "*My younger brother, there,*" said Raama, "*the one who laughs all day, will surely make a better husband for you. He is all alone in this place while I already have a wife.*"

The she-demon looked Lakshmana up and down and thought: "*He isn't a bad-looking fellow.*" So off she went to try and tempt him with even more fantastical stories of the places she would show him: where the paths were covered with emerald stones, where mountains were made of boulders of sugar, where wine flowed in lakes, where parrots knew sixteen languages and told stories in all of them.

But Lakshmana just laughed and laughed at these tales. He shook his head. "*I would be a very poor catch, indeed, while Raama is still around. Go back to him and don't take no for an answer.*"

The she-demon was starting to get a bit angry now. Her body began to tremble and quiver as she returned to Raama, heat waves following in her footsteps. She stood before him, hands on hips and said: *"This is your last chance for a good life. Get rid of that stupid wife of yours and come with me. She's ugly, lazy and a real feather-brain from the looks of it. I, on the other hand, am sister to a powerful king."*

"How dare you speak of me like that," said Seeta.

That was the last straw for the she-demon. She uttered the most horrible shriek and threw off her disguise as a beautiful woman and stood there breathing out smoke from her nostrils. Lakshmana stiffened.

Raama pushed Seeta behind him. The she-demon clawed the dust with her scaly green feet. She stretched her fingers wide and sharp black claws sprung out.

"The woman dies," she hissed through evil, rotting teeth. Then she spread her arms and charged straight towards Seeta's throat.

Seeta screamed.

Lakshmana, swift as a swallow, dropped to one knee and sent an arrow humming towards the hag. It hit her straight on the nose, cutting off its end.

The she-demon screamed and screamed, clutching her bleeding nose and ran wildly off into the bushes. *"You're all dead!"* she screamed. *"Dead! Dead."*

Then all went silent again. The sun had set. Night had arrived.

Hanumaan stopped speaking. He was quite out of breath.

The boy stared at him, eyes almost popping. "The nose," he said. "Aunt Sissey's nose . . . !"

Hanumaan nodded. "That's why I had to tell you what happened in the story."

"Are you telling us that Aunt Sissey is a she-demon?" asked the girl in a voice filling with fear.

"I'm only telling you a story," said Hanumaan.

"What did the woman in the story do?" asked the boy.

"Well . . . I did tell you that she was the sister of Raavana, the powerful Lord of the Dark Force, didn't I?" said Hanumaan.

The children nodded.

80

"And I did tell you that he had some really fierce and cruel brothers, didn't I?" said Hanumaan.

The children shook their heads. "No, you didn't."

"Ah, well, in fact Raavana had some really fierce and cruel brothers," said Hanumaan. He scratched his tiny head and looked into the mirror. He looked around the dressing table as if he'd lost something. "You don't happen to have any walnuts by any chance, do you?" he said.

"Hanumaan!" shouted both children together. "What happened next?"

Hanumaan sat down again and continued...

THE SHE-DEMON, sister of Raavana, flew screaming through the forest and banged on the door of her other evil and cruel brothers. They took one look at her face, heard her side of the story and became black with fury.

"We'll kill that puny mortal!" they roared and sent a soldier into all the darkest places of the forest to gather together an army of fourteen thousand of the ugliest, most wicked and most nasty Night Rangers that had ever been seen in the place.

The dark army set off towards Raama's camp. It was such a terrible force that the whole forest shook beneath their feet. There were elephants, snakes, strange two-headed birds pulling flying chariots, and soldiers carrying spears and clubs and chains and javelins with foul green poison on their tips.

They made even the fiercest animals of the forest run for shelter. Behind them trees were being torn from their roots and the sheer weight of the army pressed deep hollows into the skin of the earth which turned black and as hard as rock after they passed — nothing would grow in that place again.

Finally they came to the foot of the mountain where Raama lived. They sent out a spy — a tiny creature that had

three eyes, webbed feet and a terrible skin which was full of
bleeding sores. But he was fast and light like quicksilver. He
darted from tree to tree, swinging between the branches
sometimes or leaping into the air and floating on the high
breezes. He finally reached a small hill from where he could
see Raama's hut.

He counted three people standing outside it. Then he saw
the tall one tell the woman to go back into the hut and the
younger one rushing around the yard sticking clumps of
arrows here, sticking spears there, swords in another place.
Soon the whole yard was bristling with weapons sticking up
like dangerous bushes.

The spy reported back to the generals of the army of the
Dark Force. When they heard that the enemy was made up
of two young men and one woman, they laughed their ugly
laughs, purple breath escaping from their rotting mouths.

"We don't need the whole army for this," they said. *"We
fourteen generals can finish the matter in ten minutes."*

They climbed onto the backs of strange dark birds and
took off into the night sky, heading towards Raama's hut.

Suddenly the door to the bedroom slammed open. The girl tossed a flannel
over the tiny Hanumaan on the dressing table. The boy jumped back into
bed.

Aunt Sissey took one look at the window pane broken by Hanumaan's
dramatic entry, and one look at the boy who had jumped onto the bed, and
said: "I saw that, young man. Soon I won't have to put up with your nonsense
any more."

"What are you talking about?" said the boy.

"How did that window pane get broken?" asked Aunt Sissey. "And before
you invent one of your stories, I saw the guilty way you jumped onto the
bed when I walked in. I don't miss a thing, you know."

"He didn't break the window," said the girl.

"So, young madam, I wondered when you were going to show your true colours," said Aunt Sissey.

Her nose looked swollen and dark bruises had started to spread under her eyes, giving them a wild look. Then, without another word, she left the room. The girl quickly lifted the flannel, but Hanumaan too had gone.

Outside the morning sun had risen and threatened to bake the earth. The children stayed in their room for the rest of the day.

Day 10
The Dark Force attacks

THE CHILDREN WOKE EARLY. From Aunt Sissey's anger of the day before they knew that trouble was not far off.

They had spent the rest of the previous day in their room talking about the strange events of the past. Never in their wildest dreams could they have imagined that they'd meet a monkey like Hanumaan. Sometimes he was so like a monkey, especially when he was upset and pretended that they were not there and scratched behind his ears or ate his sweets without looking at them. Sometimes he would frighten them when he puffed up his fur and drew his lips back in a snarl to display pink gums and yellowing fangs. But then he was gentle again and the girl wanted to put her arms around him.

While they had been talking about these things, the bedroom door had burst open for the second time that day and Aunt Sissey had appeared. "I just thought you'd like to know that your father wasn't too pleased when I told him about your behaviour," she had said. "He's on his way down to take you back home."

"Him and fourteen generals, I expect," said the boy. Aunt Sissey said, *humph!* and slammed the door. The boy had wondered what Raama was going to do . . .

The night had passed without any more bad news and now the tenth day was dawning. Hanumaan blew in on a misty morning breeze.

The story of Raama continued . . .

THE SMELL OF BATTLE filled the wind. Fourteen generals of the Dark Force were heading towards the tiny hut on the mountainside. Their minds were full of hate and death.

Raama told Lakshmana to take Seeta to the safety of a cave in the mountainside and stay there to protect her. Lakshmana didn't want to go at first, but he knew from the iron in Raama's voice that he had no choice. Seeta began to cry and Lakshmana led her away.

Raama was all alone in the camp. His hearing told him that this time the battle was going to be a fierce one — the sounds of the troops of the Dark Forces were wild in their war chants: bellowing, grunting, roaring, whooping. The beasts and creatures they rode were just as ugly in their sounds and looks, some with three eyes, some with rotten skin hanging off, some with teeth which were orange with dirt.

Raama first washed his body slowly, feeling the cool water
on his arms and chest, drops of water trickling slowly down
the muscles of his arms and torso like rivers gently winding
their way through a hilly land. Then he rubbed oil over it to
make it easier for his armour to slide on. The sounds of mad
horn-blowing and the shouting and drumming of the enemy
got nearer. Raama could see a huge cloud of dust now,
telling him that thousands of Night Rangers were on their
way to his hut.

Yet, without any haste, he walked around the yard,
checking the weapons that Lakshmana had planted. The
feathers on one of the arrow shafts was coming loose, so he
neatly tied it back with a blade of grass. He picked up one of
the javelins with explosive heads and tested its point of
balance — he knew it would surely bring death to its target
like a thunderbolt. He looked back at the hut that he shared
with Seeta. A water pot had been dropped in Seeta's haste to
get away and Raama carefully picked up the pieces, one by
one, and placed them to one side.

It was time to put his armour on — it felt cool to the
touch.

With unswerving attention, he did up the twenty-one
buckles and then slipped on the silver wrist bands. In full
battle dress he looked as splendid as the sun at midday. His
long black hair was tied in a knot at the back. He picked up
a handful of red dust and rubbed his palms in it and clapped.
He remembered the day when he was very young and his
father took him to to the sacred field just outside the city.
And while his father had ploughed the soil, he had played in
the dust by the side of the furrows, clapping up tiny clouds of
dust. Then an image of the face of Seeta, daughter of the

Earth, filled his mind and all thoughts died away.

Raama was ready to fight.

WITH THE BLARE OF TRUMPETS and booms of drums, the fourteen generals of the Dark Forces burst through the trees upon the lone prince. Before he had time to move, their arrows showered down on him, piercing his armour and sticking out of him like a porcupine's spines. He sprang back to his feet and, with a powerful sweep of his arm, snapped off the arrows sticking in his chest plate. He let fly three javelins all together. They hit their targets in the air, bursting sparks high and wild, bringing down three generals, dead.

Raama's bow now came into action. Flights of arrows flew from its string so fast that smoke started to rise from it. General after general hit the dust, stung by the arrows of Raama that hissed through the air like deadly cobras. Raama moved furiously, cutting into the generals like a mighty tornado, scattering bodies to his left and to his right, till there was not one general left.

Watching all this from the trees was the slimy spy of the Dark Force. So shocked was he to see how easily Raama had defeated the generals that he lost his balance and came crashing to the ground just six feet from Raama. They both stared at one another for a moment and then Raama placed a deadly arrow into his bow string and drew back. But, with a TWANG, the string snapped.

The slimy green spy took one look at Raama, thanked his luck, turned and charged into the bushes. He arrived back at the evil camp breathless and covered in dust and blood.

WHEN RAAVANA'S BROTHERS heard of what had happened they became wild with rage. And when they heard that they had lost all their generals, they yelled for their chariots, screamed battle orders, and fourteen thousand Night Rangers — crack troops of the Dark Force — thundered down on Raama's camp led by Raavana's brothers.

Imagine the scene from high up with the gods in heaven . . .

See one man standing alone against fourteen thousand screaming, spitting, swearing monsters. His mind concentrated, his heart steady, his body and arms and legs moving so fast that you can hardly see them for dust. Arrows flying, horns blaring, bodies, blood, spears, clubs, clashing, dashing, dying, screaming. And in the midst of all this, silent, moving like death through the army of the Dark Force was Raama. Deadly. Calm. Strong. Blood was flowing from thousands of wounds on his body, but it made him look even more splendid, like forest trees in full red blossom at sunset.

He didn't stop till nearly every one of the fourteen thousand Night Rangers were dead. There were just two left — the brothers of Raavana, Lord of the Dark Forces, King of the Night Rangers. They stood facing Raama across the thousands of bodies covering the mountain side. *"What you have done to our sister and what you have done here is terrible,"* they said. *"Who are you really?"*

"I am death to all that is evil in the world," said Raama and he let fly a two-headed arrow with tips like crescent moons. The arrow sliced off the heads of the two Night Rangers and their heavy bodies dropped to the ground.

Raama sunk to his knees and bowed his head in prayer.

A sweet rain fell from heaven. It tasted of life. It washed the wounds on Raama's body and tiny rivulets of blood trickled their way from the camp down to the lake, washing the earth of the deadly scene.

Lakshmana and Seeta came out of the cave and picked their way though the mountain of dead bodies. They looked like people who were walking in their sleep. Seeta saw her husband, on his knees, hundreds of arrows sticking out of his arms and legs and chest and back and neck and shoulders. She screamed: *"RAAMA!"* and rushed over to him.

Peace entered Raama's heart and he shut his eyes. He felt the weapons being removed, one at a time, from his body, making him full of light. Then he felt Seeta's tiny hands unbuckle his armour with fingers that moved as gently as butterflies. And then the touch of cool water mixed with a paste of healing herbs. Raama knew that there was nowhere to go and nothing to do — Seeta was with him, her tears washing him, cleaning his wound of all poison.

The children were totally silent at this point in the story.

Through the window came the sound of a car pulling into the front drive. The door-bell rang and they heard the sound of voices — Aunt Sissey's, Dad's and Mum's. The children couldn't hear exactly what was being said but words like, "your poor nose . . . just wait till I see him . . . that's terrible . . ." drifted into the room.

"Hanumaan, tell us what to do," pleaded the girl.

"Choose the right weapons," said Hanumaan and then he leapt onto the wind and was gone.

The door to the bedroom opened. Dad was there, behind him Mum and Aunt Sissey. The boy remembered the picture of Raama waiting before the battle, how calm he was, how he checked his weapons, how he put on his armour. Gradually his heart stopped beating with fear. A puff of breeze tossed the curtains and fresh wind filled the room, gently cooling his hair.

"I'm sorry," he heard himself say.

"Is that all?" said his father, with fire in his voice.

"Sometimes I do things without thinking," said the boy. A single clear, bright tear rolled down his cheek. "It's as if I'm not myself. I never really want to do those things, but I always find myself in trouble. I really am sorry, but sometimes I don't know how to say it."

The girl looked at him standing there alone and she too found hot tears burning her cheeks. Her father told the boy to sit down on the stool by the window and asked everyone else to leave the room. Father and son seemed to be in there for ages; sometimes voices would be raised.

From the garden the girl could see the room with its open window and broken window pane. Fragrance from the hyacinths made her dizzy and then she could smell the grass, the earth, the apples, everything around and all her tears stopped.

Without taking her eyes off the window, she walked backwards down the garden till she could see the boy in the room. He was sitting quite still and speaking from time to time without movement. The girl felt quite at peace now. She turned to the goldfish pond and saw something that made her jump: standing beside the fishing gnome, and not much larger, was Hanumaan.

He smiled at her and said: "He's doing well. He has brought down the Demon Anger, the Demon Fear, the Demon Untruth, the Demon Dream. Some came in with your father, some were hiding in the heart of the boy. He is winning this battle; there will be others."

"But Dad will take us home soon. Will you be there?" asked the girl.

"Of course I will," said Hanumaan. "Soon I will enter the story and meet the glorious Raama. Oh, what adventures we had together."

Saying that, Hanumaan shot high into the clouds and vanished.

Day 11
Raavana's evil plan

NO ONE SPOKE on the drive back home. The children felt a bit lost being so far from the park with its secret grove of poplars. Their own garden was tiny compared to Aunt Sissey's. It didn't seem the right place to meet Hanumaan. Each time they felt a breeze they thought that he had come, each time the curtains moved they thought that he was there. The air was all around them — Hanumaan could be anywhere.

"He said he'll come when we call him," said the girl. "Let's try."

"Hanumaan! Hanumaan!" they called from their bedroom window. A few stray cats were in the garden, sniffing around the guinea pig hutch, but no sign of Hanumaan. The boy shut the window and turned back with a sigh. What he saw made him jump.

There on the rug was Hanumaan, sitting as usual, this time the size of a normal monkey!

"It's not bad," Hanumaan said, looking around the room. "A bit messy, but not bad."

The children quickly started to clear the mess, picking up books by the armful, scooping up the lego pieces, stuffing jumpers into drawers. "Would you like me to hoover the carpet? Would that make it any better?" said the girl.

"It's perfectly fine as it is," said Hanumaan. "Just sit down and listen. Or if you want to be Mr Tidy and Little Miss Mop, carry on and call me when you're ready." He rose to leave, but the girl grabbed him by the arm and told him to stay and continue the story.

"Where did we get to . . . ?" asked Hanumaan, scratching his ear and with a sly twinkle in his eye.

"The battle!" said the boy.

"Ah yes . . . the battle . . . fourteen thousand killed. What's next . . . ?"

WHEN THE WICKED SISTER of Raavana heard that her brothers and fourteen thousand troops had been killed by Raama alone, she became mad with anger. She grabbed her hair and pulled it so hard that it tore out in huge fistfuls. There was only one thing left for her to do and that was to tell Raavana himself about what had happened.

Covering her face with a black veil and carrying a bundle wrapped in cloth, she arrived at Raavana's golden city in the place called Lanka. She pushed her way past foul-smelling guards to Raavana's private rooms. She tore back the veil from her face and showed Raavana her nose (or what was left of it). Then she threw down the bundle of cloth she was carrying: out rolled the heads of their brothers. There was silence for a moment and then Raavana, Lord of the Dark Force, exploded in fury. His anger shook the golden palace so much that it nearly fell to the ground. *"Who did this to you?"* he roared. *"And who has killed my brothers? And why didn't their army help them?"*

"The whole army has been destroyed — all fourteen thousand of them," said his sister. *"And that's not all — holy men are moving back to the Dandaka forest and are making offerings to the gods. And our people are too frightened to pour blood on their fires as we used to do."*

"Who has done this?" hissed Raavana.

"Raama, a prince from Ayodhya," said his sister, *"and his brother Lakshmana, the one who shot off my nose."*

Raavana was ready to rise up there and then, kill Raama and Lakshmana with his own bare hands and then bite off their heads. But his sister stopped him. *"There is one way you can destroy him,"* she said, *"and that is to steal his beautiful wife Seeta. Without her, Raama will surely die."*

"*Right*," said Raavana. "*That's what we will do.*"

FIRST THEY NEEDED A PLAN, so Raavana went off
to see his uncle, a magician of the Dark Force who had
great powers. When the magician heard the story he
became worried and begged Raavana to go back home. "*I
know these princes,*" he said and blinked and cleared his
throat. "*These are the very two princes who, when they were
fifteen years old, helped the most powerful sage in the land to
complete his sacrifice. These two young scrawny things managed to
stop hundreds of powerful Night Rangers from pouring blood over
the offerings.*"

"*Who told you these lies?*" said Raavana.

The magician swallowed hard and said: "*Nobody needs to
tell me the story — I was one of those Night Rangers. The blow
from Raama's arrow sent me flying one thousand miles, dumping
me in the sea. Ever since then I've lived a quiet life here,
practising the art of magic. I don't want to tangle with him
again. Forget your plan.*"

These words made Raavana furious. He grabbed the old
man by the neck and lifted him off the ground and said:
"*You will help me defeat this wretched man or I shall smash you
into the ground and turn your bones to dust.*"

Raavana's uncle trembled with fear and thought: "*If I
don't help Raavana, he will kill me and I'll end up in hell. If I
do help, Raama will kill me and, who knows, I might end up in
heaven.*"

"*Okay, I'll help,*" he said.

This was Raavana's plan: the magician was to turn himself
into an enchanted golden deer and trick Raama into
following him into the forest. And when Raama was away,

Raavana could swoop in on his fiery chariot and grab Seeta.

"Let's do it," said Raavana.

THE TWO EVIL NIGHT RANGERS, full of the Dark Force, put their plan into action. They arrived at Raama's camp just as the sun was about to set. The magician turned himself into a beautiful golden deer with antlers sparkling with rubies and hoofs studded with diamonds. The moment Seeta saw the golden deer, she wanted it. *"We'll be going home soon,"* she pleaded with Raama. *"Wouldn't it be wonderful if we took an animal as beautiful as this back with us to the City?"*

Above the hut Lakshmana saw black crows flying in front of the setting sun — cawing wildly and fighting over the flesh of a baby deer. The evening air was thick with purple clouds full of poisonous rain. Thunder rumbled loud and near. Slimy creatures started to crawl out of holes in the soil and slither into the bushes. The wind was full of the sounds of screeching birds and scavenging beasts. And shining and twinkling in the middle of all this darkness was the golden deer.

"Don't go," said Lakshmana. *"Let's kill the creature now — it's obviously a trick."*

"I'll try to capture it alive for Seeta," said Raama. *"But if it looks as if that's not possible, have no fear, I will show the creature no mercy. Whatever happens, on NO account are you to take your eyes off Seeta, even for a moment."*

Lakshmana promised that he would guard Seeta with his life.

The deer darted into the forest and Raama ran swiftly after it. Deeper and deeper into the forest ran the deer. Each time Raama was about to get his hands on it, it would vanish and then reappear further away. In this way Raama was drawn far from the camp and he knew that he was being tricked.

He stopped running and stood his ground. The deer stopped too, sniffing the air, trembling with fear because the wind carried the scent of death. The deer turned to run away again. But, swift as lightning, Raama let fly an arrow straight into its heart. The enchanted deer fell to the ground and slowly all the gold and jewels started to melt, leaving the ugly form of the wizard squirming in the mud.

Then the wizard played his last evil trick. He copied Raama's voice exactly and shouted out: *"Help, Seeta! Help, Lakshmana! Help me!"*

BACK IN THE CAMP Seeta heard Raama's voice calling for help. It was a sound she had never heard before and fear chilled her bones to the marrow. How could her brave hero be in trouble?

"Lakshmana, do you hear that?" she said, her voice trembling like leaves in a high wind. *"Raama is in trouble. You must help him."*

"I heard," said Lakshmana, *"but I am uneasy. It feels like another trick of the Night Rangers."*

"Please go to your brother. He is calling to you for help," pleaded Seeta.

But Lakshmana shook his head. *"Raama instructed me to stay here and here is where I'm going to stay,"* he said.

Seeta became even more upset. She began to wring her hands and tear at her clothes. *"Why are you not going to help?"* she cried.

"Dear Seeta, be calm," said Lakshmana. *"Do you not realise that all these years in the forest you have been safe because Raama*

95

was at your side. Now that you have sent him off, he has left me here in his place to protect you. Do not send me away as well!"

Seeta's eyes became red with anger and tears. *"That's not the truth,"* she screamed. *"The truth is that you want Raama dead so that you can have me for your wife and you can take his kingdom!"*

The words struck Lakshmana deeply and he almost fell to the ground. *"You are Raama's wife,"* he said. *"I would never even dream of doing the things you say. In all the time since leaving Ayodhya I have never so much as looked at your face directly — my eyes have always been cast down at your feet. So how can I want you for my wife?"*

"Then the only explanation must be that you won't rush to Raama's help because you are a coward," said Seeta, her face glowing red hot.

"Raama does not need my help," said Lakshmana. *"Why do you forget his true strength? Wasn't it Raama who killed the fourteen thousand demons single-handed just a few days ago? Do you think a mere deer can be the cause of danger to such a hero?"*

"Go away!" screamed Seeta. *"You are a coward. Leave me here alone, because the protection of a coward is no protection."*

Lakshmana, stung by her hard words, said: *"As you please. I will go after Raama, but it is against my better judgement."*

With a heavy heart, he picked up his bow and arrow. Using the end of his bow he drew a large a circle in the dust around the hut. *"With Raama and me away, this circle is your only protection,"* he said to Seeta. *"You are not to step out of the circle because, outside it, there is nothing to keep you safe!"*

Then he turned and ran off to look for his brother.

Unknown to Lakshmana, the whole scene was being spied

upon by a dark presence in the bushes. This was the moment that the evil Raavana had been waiting for . . .

Hanumaan stopped speaking because he noticed that the girl was starting to look frightened. "Everyone needs protection," he said in a gentle voice. "There is always protection to hand. But the trick is to make use of it."

"But surely . . ." began the girl. But Hanumaan stopped her words.

"Think on what I have said. Don't drive it away by saying 'but surely'. I'll be back tomorrow." And Hanumaan was off.

Day 12
Raavana kidnaps Seeta

THE GIRL WASN'T SURE if she agreed with Hanumaan when he said that there was always protection all around. What she disliked even more was the way he didn't let her speak. All she was going to say was: "But surely, young people today are much more grown up and need to learn how to look after *themselves* and it is not necessary for others to tell you what to do."

It was no use speaking to her brother either, because all he kept saying was: "Trust Hanumaan."

"That's all very easy for you to say," said the girl, "but where's the big danger?"

"Raavana," said the boy.

"But surely Raama is strong enough to kill him," said the girl.

"Then Raama will keep you safe."

"But he's only someone in a story," said the girl, "and so is Raavana. So stop trying to get me all mixed up!"

The boy shrugged. "He certainly helped me when Dad was so angry. All I had to do was remember how calm he was when the Night Rangers attacked him and that made me calm."

The girl didn't speak to the boy after that. And when Hanumaan arrived to continue the story, she was still not speaking.

Hanumaan ignored the frosty silence and began to speak...

WITH RAAMA AND LAKSHMANA OUT OF THE WAY, there was only the magic circle in the dust to keep Seeta from danger. Raavana knew that all he had to do was to get her to step outside the circle. So, using magic, he disguised himself as a poor old monk, staggered out of the trees and dropped to the ground — just outside the magic circle in the dust. *"Help a poor old man,"* he cried. *"Water, food . . . please have pity on a man of God."*

Seeta appeared at the door of the hut and Raavana saw for the first time her full beauty. Even in her moment of distress, her face was like the moon reflected in a tranquil pool. He knew that he had to steal her and make her his wife. *"Please lady,"* he cried. *"Water for a dying man . . ."*

Without thinking, Seeta grabbed a water pot and a mug and rushed over to him. The moment her foot stepped out of the magic circle, Raavana threw off his disguise and showed his true form as the King of the Dark Force. He was as huge as a mountain, his eyes red as fire, his arms as thick as tree trunks. There were moments when from his neck sprang out ten heads and from his shoulders sprang out twenty arms and then they disappeared.

"I have come for you," he whispered and grabbed Seeta by the hair and started to drag her into the bushes. Then he gave a piercing whistle and his fiery chariot shot out of the sky. Seeta screamed for help but Raama was too far away to hear. Raavana put his hand over Seeta's mouth and dragged her into the chariot and, with a flick of his whip, the horses charged and lifted off into the air.

Seeta was screaming and crying and begging Raavana to let her go. *"I am the wife of Raama,"* she cried. *"He will kill you for doing this terrible deed."*

Raavana's ten heads and twenty arms shot out and all his mouths were laughing. *"Know who I truly am,"* he said. *"I am Raavana, Lord of the Dark Force, ruler of the Night Rangers. Even the gods fear me because they cannot harm me. Do you really think that I am afraid of a puny little man?"*

"Why are you doing this terrible thing?" screamed Seeta.

"Your Raama and his brother have cut off my sister's nose, have killed my brothers, have slaughtered my fourteen best generals and have destroyed fourteen thousand of my best troops. Now they have killed my uncle . . . And you dare ask me why I am doing this?" roared Raavana.

"But they were wicked," said Seeta.

"And your Raama who has killed so many is a saint, I suppose," said Raavana and he whipped his horses to fly higher and faster. Seeta's screams could no longer be heard from the ground.

BUT HIGH up above the clouds circled a lone figure who saw everything. It was the mighty vulture king, Jataayu, who had promised to guard Seeta from harm. Folding back his wings and pointing his sharp beak downwards, he dropped like a thunderbolt out of the heavens, aimed straight at Raavana's chariot.

Raavana was taken by surprise at the speed of the great vulture. He reached for his arrow, but Jataayu's huge wings shattered the bow to pieces. The vulture rose again into the clouds and Raavana lost him for a moment. Then, screeching with fury, Jataayu plunged at the chariot once more and knocked one of the fiery horses so hard that the animal hung dead in the harness, dragging the chariot earthwards.

Again and again the brave Jataayu swooped, smashing the wheels of the chariot and smashing Raavana's weapons out of his hand. But then, the mighty vulture's foot got tangled in the reins of the chariot.

With two powerful blows, Raavana cut off Jataayu's wings.

Seeta screamed: *"JATAAYU!"* as the brave vulture king dropped like a stone, crashing through the trees and landing with a thud on the forest floor.

Raavana pointed his chariot south and flew off. Seeta began to struggle and tried to jump out, but Raavana grabbed her by the hair and shoved her to the floor. *"You are going to be my wife,"* he roared.

"Never!" she screamed and, tore off her necklace and threw it away, then her bangles and her veil. From the earth below no one could hear her cries, but some monkeys standing on a hill saw the jewels fall from the sky and scampered over to pick them up.

The chariot flew on, through rain clouds and warm skies, over forests and meadows, over lakes shimmering with fish and flamingoes, over mountains so high that they seemed to touch the moon. Finally they crossed a wide ocean with huge waves, and landed in Raavana's fortress kingdom of Lanka.

Raavana, who had been so harsh and cruel to Seeta, suddenly changed. He took off his armour and put on fine silk robes. His voice became gentle and sweet. Beautiful she-demons ran down the palace steps to greet him, showering him and Seeta with rose petals. This did not seem like the city of Night Rangers — it was beautiful. The only difference was that the houses, instead of being white and cool, were made of red stone.

Raavana bowed to Seeta and said: *"Will you enter my home. My servants will give you everything you wish for."*

Seeta turned her eyes to the ground and wept. *"Then let your servants take me back to my Lord, Raama."*

"NEVER!" roared Raavana, but then he took on his

gentle voice again. *"Beautiful lady, your brightness lights up this kingdom of ours. I want you to be my wife."*

"I would rather die," said Seeta.

Raavana turned away in anger. *"Suit yourself,"* he said and clapped his hands. The beautiful girls of the palace threw off their disguise and Seeta found herself surrounded by ugly old hags. *"Take her to the Ashoka Gardens on the outskirts of the city and keep her there till she changes her mind,"* said Raavana. Then he added: *"I want to warn all of you, no one is to lay a finger on her or they will be devoured by me. Now go!"*

Seeta cried to the heavens: *"RAAMA! SAVE ME!"*

SEETA'S VOICE seemed to enter straight into the heart of Raama who was still in the forest many thousand miles away. He dropped to his knee as if he had been shot by a poison arrow. When he opened his eyes he saw his brother Lakshmana running like a rabbit trough the trees, leaping over roots and ducking branches, bow in hand.

"What are you doing here?" cried Raama. Lakshmana told Raama what had happened. Raama just said: *"Seeta's in trouble."* And the two of them took off through the forest, swift as panthers.

When they reached the camp they saw the signs of struggle. They saw Seeta's garland lying in the dust and the flowers from her hair all trampled. Raama called and called her name. He was so angry with Lakshmana for leaving her alone and unprotected. Poor Lakshmana was heartbroken too. They both called out Seeta's name again and again, rushing this way and that — into the hut, up to the cave, down to the lake, into the vegetable garden. No Seeta.

Raama was wild with grief now. He grabbed as many

weapons as he could carry and ran crying into the forest, followed by his brother.

His foot stepped on a soft dark shape on the forest floor and, thinking that it was another Night Ranger, lifted his sword to kill it. But a feeble voice arose: *"Raama, don't . . . it's me."* Raama came to his senses again.

It was the mighty Jataayu, the powerful vulture, lying there dying with both wings cut off. He told Raama all that had happened. *"The evil Raavana who grabbed your gentle wife Seeta is heading south."* Then the mighty Jataayu, uttering Raama's name on his last breath, died.

Raama and Lakshmana built a huge fire in a clearing in the forest and placed Jataayu's body on it. The two princes bowed their heads and prayed for the safe passage of Jataayu's soul. The fire crackled and spat sparks high into the night sky where they mingled with the stars and then snuffed out.

The forest that night was as silent as a grave.

Hanumaan fell silent. The children watched his tiny face. A tear rolled from his eye. The girl began to sob.

Hanumaan said: "I think you should carry on clearing your room now, don't you?" He looked directly at the girl.

"Yes, yes, I think we should," she agreed, having completely forgotten that she did not want to speak to anyone.

"Tomorrow" said Hanumaan, "I will tell you of a happier event — the day I finally saw Raama with my own eyes and heard his voice with my own ears and carried him on my own shoulders. Yes . . . that was a happy day."

Before the children could say another word, the monkey was on the window ledge and then he was gone.

Day 13
Raama meets Hanumaan

THE NEXT DAY, the children were left on their own at home. Their father had prepared a timetable for the day and gave them many tasks to do around the house. They had to clean the front room, change the flowers in all the vases, scrub down the cooker, do their homework.

He said: "I don't want to come home, tired after work, and find that you've been watching television."

The children gave their word and kept it. Housework was really hard, especially when they tried to do it well. By the time the afternoon arrived, there were more things on the kitchen floor than there had been when they started. The boy had decided to tidy the food cupboard properly, had taken everything out, scrubbed down the shelves and thrown away old packets of spaghetti and a stale bag of crisps. But he got too tired to finish the job. All he wanted to do was have a rest.

Just then the french windows to the garden blew open and Hanumaan stood before them. Across one shoulder was draped a flowing saffron shawl. "Let's stop now," he said, "and refresh our weary hearts."

The children sat in the middle of all the food and listened...

AFTER THE TWO PRINCES had scattered the ashes of Jataayu in the river, Raama said that he wanted to leave immediately to follow the trail south. The brothers gathered together their weapons and entered the forest which was black with sadness. Snakes slithered across their path. Ravens cawed. Everything was covered in dark slime. But Raama and Lakshmana hardly noticed the change.

Deeper and deeper into the darkness they went, hacking down creepers and vines that blocked the way. The only sounds were the toads and insects that creaked and chirruped and hummed and buzzed, that and the sound of the mighty princes hacking their way through the trees. Then, suddenly, there was a ROAAAR!

Without stopping to think or to look, Raama and Lakshmana both sent shining arrows spitting like angry fire towards the sound. Another roar followed by a howl of pain told them that they had hit their target. Raama's sword was in his hand in a flash and he charged through the black forest, leaping over fallen trees, dodging vines, and came to the body of a massive creature with long arms and a huge mouth right in the middle of his belly. Two arrows were sticking out of his chest. Raama raised his sword to finish off the job, but the creature groaned: *"Are you Raama, mighty prince of the kingdom, banished into the forest with his wife Seeta and good brother Lakshmana . . . ?"*

"I am," said Raama. *"But now you must . . ."*

"Please kill me," cried out the creature. *"My curse will be lifted when I am killed by Raama. That's what the witch who gave me this horrible shape said. But before you kill me listen to what I must say."*

"It's a trick, Raama," shouted Lakshmana. *"Kill him now!"* But Raama, placing one foot on the creature's neck, asked for his message.

"Many miles south of here you will find a beautiful valley. In it lives the exiled king of all monkeys, Sugreeva. Go to him, help him. He is destined to help you get Seeta back," the creature's voice grew faint. *"Now fast, kill me!"* Raama plunged the sword into the creature's heart and from the wound hissed bright blue smoke, rising and rising till the princes could make out the form a handsome young man. He waved to

them and, in a trail of blue sparks, shot straight towards the third heaven.

IT WAS EXACTLY AS THE CREATURE HAD DESCRIBED. South of the dark forest the trees opened up and the princes found themselves looking out across a beautiful green plane with mountains in the background. The scent of a million different flowers and fruit was like a balm to their hearts. White birds circled the lake and then landed on the clear blue water, one after the other, like feathers, hardly causing a ripple. A flock of antelopes grazed peacefully and far above the scene a single hawk floated on the high currents of air.

Lakshmana then noticed that, instead of being happy, tears were rolling down Raama's cheeks and the glorious prince had thrown down his weapons. Lakshmana tried to comfort his brother, but Raama said: *"Wouldn't this place have made Seeta happy? Each week, each day, each hour, each fraction of time she is away makes my heart heavier. My mind feels like it is full of millions of demons, shouting and screaming and laughing at my sorrow. But where is Seeta now? I despair of ever finding her. And who is this monkey king, Sugreeva? How can a mere monkey help us when we have the strength to send thousands of Night Rangers to the jaws of death?"*

Lakshmana tried to cheer Raama up by pointing out all the beauty around them. Across the lake there were blue mountains that seemed to touch the clouds. And from the mountains drifted hundreds of waterfalls that made it look as if it was decorated by blue ribbons of water. And when the wind grew stronger, the waterfalls would all blow spray high into the sky making hundreds of rainbows.

"*Look, Raama,*" said Lakshmana. "*The trees are groaning with fruit and nectar. Let us rest our tired bodies. Let us bathe in the pools below the waterfalls. Let us swim with the fish.*" But nothing Lakshmana said could lift Raama's sadness.

SUDDENLY THE WIND grew stronger and the trees were being tossed this way and that. Fruit was knocked off the branches and dropped like bombs all around the princes. Raama looked up at the trees and there on a branch high up he saw a monkey.

With one leap the monkey was on the ground. He joined his long black palms together and bowed to the princes. "*Welcome strangers,*" he said. "*You are dressed in the clothes of the hermits, yet you carry weapons. You carry no possessions and yet you have the straight backs and steady eyes of princes. Tell me who you are.*"

Raama smiled for the first time in days. "*This monkey has a fine way of speaking,*" he said to Lakshmana. Then turning to the monkey, he said: "*I am Raama, prince of Ayodhya, sent into exile for fourteen years with my brother Lakshmana and wife Seeta. We have lived in the forests for many happy years, but now that beautiful lady Seeta has been stolen from me by the Dark Force. Now tell me who you are — you who look like a monkey, but speak like a courtier.*"

The monkey bowed. "*I am chief minister to Sugreeva, the monkey king in exile.*"

Raama and Lakshmana exchanged quick glances. "*Did you say Sugreeva?*" asked Lakshmana.

"*Yes he is, my master. He too has had his kingdom stolen from him and now lives in the blue mountains across the lake,"* said the monkey.

"He is the one we have come to meet," said Lakshmana.

The monkey smiled. *"I think he will be very pleased to meet you. We have heard stories of the mighty Raama and brave Lakshmana. Come with me."*

Then, right before their very eyes, the monkey started to grow and grow till he was the size of a giant oak tree. He lifted the princes onto his shoulders as if they were as light as leaves and, with one bound, leapt across the lake and landed on the top of the mountain.

"That was some leap!" cried Lakshmana.

"Thank you," said the monkey and he bowed to them. *"Now I must find my master, Sugreeva."* He turned to go but Raama stopped him and said: *"You haven't told us your name."*

"I am Hanumaan, son of the Lord of the Wind, at the service of Raama," said the monkey.

THE CAMP OF SUGREEVA, the monkey king in exile, was full of monkeys and bears who had followed their king into the mountains. They lived off honey and fruit, nuts and nectar. Life on the mountain was kind. Raama and Lakshmana stood on the edge of a giant waterfall, its water plunging thousands of feet into the beautiful lake below. There they waited for Sugreeva.

The monkey king, followed by his ministers, approached the princes. *"From one king to another, greetings,"* said Sugreeva.

Raama bowed. *"I was told that you can help me find my wife Seeta who has been stolen from me,"* he said.

Sugreeva clapped his hands and one of his ministers handed him a bundle wrapped in banana leaves. This he handed to Raama. The mighty hero slowly undid the wrapping and there in his hands were Seeta's veil and necklace. *"Where did you get these?"* asked Raama.

"A few months ago, some friends and I were taking the evening air on the top of this very mountain. And as we stood peacefully admiring the dying colours of the sun, the sky was torn open by the fierce screams of a Night Ranger's chariot speeding southward. We were certain that from it came the cries of a woman in distress. And then floating down from the chariot came the things you have in your hand."

"Point out the way," say Lakshmana. *"It sounds like we are hot on the trail."*

"What can two of you do?" asked Sugreeva. *"I, on the other hand, have an army of a million monkeys and bears, waiting on my command."*

Lakshmana looked round the camp and saw just a few hundred.

"They're not all here, of course," said Sugreeva. *"They are back in my kingdom which has been stolen from me by my powerful brother Vaali. If you help me defeat Vaali and win back my kingdom and my wife, then my whole army will help you find Seeta."*

Raama and Lakshmana looked at one another and looked around the camp. *"What do you think of them?"* whispered Raama.

"I was most impressed by that first one we met," said Lakshmana. *"I really trust Hanumaan."* Raama nodded in agreement. He reached out a hand in friendship and shook the hand of Sugreeva.

That's how Raama and Sugreeva made their pact. Raama's
face was stern. He sensed that he was close to finding Seeta
now . . . just one more task before the final battle . . .

Hanumaan stood and dusted his tail.

"You must have been really proud to hear Raama speak of you like that,"
said the girl.

"It's funny," said the monkey. "From the moment I met Raama, I became
like someone watching an actor on a stage — an actor called Hanumaan. I
watched Hanumaan jump from the tree and speak to the two princes on the
shores of that beautiful lake. I watched Hanumaan lift the princes onto his
shoulders and leap to the top of the mountain. I watched Hanumaan present
the two heroes to Sugreeva. So, in truth I wasn't proud, but Hanumaan
certainly was happy to hear the words of Raama."

"Then you must tell us the story as you saw it," said the girl.

"It's the only way the story can be told. Tomorrow you will hear of how
Raama helped Sugreeva. Hanumaan must leave you now," said the
monkey, and he was off.

Raama helps Sugreeva

THE WEATHER couldn't make up its mind the next day. The sun came out and then ducked back behind the clouds. Then it rained. And then the sun was out again. At lunchtime it was both sunny as well as rainy and a huge rainbow arched across the houses.

"Do you notice how Hanumaan's story and the weather seem to be like one another?" said the girl.

"So we should expect the story to be happy and sad, and then happy and sad all at the same time, with some hope hanging in the air?" said the boy.

"Something like that," said the girl.

"No I haven't noticed," said the boy. "But what I have noticed is that each time something terrible happens in the story, we end up in trouble and then the story tells us how to get out of it."

"So you believe that after today we'll have one more hurdle to cross and then we'll be ready to do battle with the Lord of the Dark Force to get back what's rightfully ours?" said the girl.

"Something like that," said the boy.

"I don't fancy the big battle bit," said the girl.

A voice from behind them said: "We'll just have to wait and find out which one of you is right." Hanumaan was back. The children sneaked him into their bedroom and shut the door and listened . . .

RAAMA AND SUGREEVA walked together the whole of the next day through the camp of monkeys and bears, deep in conversation. Sugreeva told him the story of how he had lost his kingdom. It happened when Sugreeva and his brother Vaali, who was massively strong, chased a terrifying monster into a deep cave. Vaali told Sugreeva to stand watch outside the cave while he went in after the monster. One hour passed, then one day, then one week. Finally, one month later there came the sound of horrible screams and a river of blood trickled out of the cave. Sugreeva was certain that Vaali had been killed and, frightened lest the monster came after him, he rolled a huge rock over the mouth of the cave and returned in deep sorrow to the kingdom. But Vaali hadn't died. He returned and accused Sugreeva of being a traitor and drove him from the kingdom.

"*So you see, Raama,*" said Sugreeva, "*though I never really meant to hurt my brother, I find myself without a proper bed to lie on — just like you. And I have lost my wife — just like you.*"

"*We must get your kingdom back,*" said Raama.

"*What? Just go up to Vaali and say: 'I'm back, so please get off my throne'?*" said Sugreeva. "*Raama, you obviously do not know my brother — he has a terrible temper and in each arm he has the strength of two hundred bull elephants.*"

Raama shut his eyes for a moment and then said: "*Tomorrow you must challenge Vaali to a fight and, while you are fighting, I'll kill him and win your kingdom back.*"

"*That's not very noble,*" said Sugreeva.

Raama said: "*This is not a question of nobility, it is a matter of destiny. I was told that Sugreeva was the one to help me get Seeta back. So I am prepared to do anything to make sure Sugreeva has all he needs for the job.*" He turned sharply and walked away saying: "*We'll meet at sunrise tomorrow.*"

EARLY THE NEXT MORNING Raama and Lakshmana woke to the sounds of the first birds. Even before the sun had appeared over the edge of the earth, the air was windless and warm. The two princes stood under one of the roaring waterfalls and felt the cooling waters thunder down on their heads. Refreshed by their shower, they sat in silent prayer till the sun was in the sky and monkeys and bears were starting to wake in the camp. All this was watched by Hanumaan from a rock outside the mouth of his cave.

Just looking at Raama in prayer made Hanumaan feel at peace. When Raama had finished his prayers Hanumaan leapt across the black boulders with fruit and honey for the princes to breakfast on. One of the young bears brought Raama his bow and he twanged it, making a noise loud enough to wake the gods in the heavens.

Sugreeva looked very jittery. He kept asking Raama if he wanted to wait till the next day, if he was sure that this was the best plan, if he was sure that his aim was good enough. Even before Sugreeva had finished speaking an arrow shot out of Raama's bow and headed straight towards a tiny pot hanging from a tree many hundred feet away. The arrow sliced through the cord and, before the pot had had time to hit the ground, three more arrows smashed it to pieces.

"I guess you're ready," said Sugreeva.

"Lead the way," said Raama, and a straggling line of monkeys and bears made their way along the twisting mountain path to the magnificent monkey kingdom of Sugreeva. They stopped at the edge of the forest outside the palace gates. Sugreeva made sure that everyone was well hidden behind the bushes and that Raama had a good view of the drawbridge. Then, boldly marching up to the gates, Sugreeva pounded on the doors and shouted: *"Vaali! Come out and fight. I want my kingdom back now!"*

When Vaali heard his brother's voice he rushed out in a burst of anger without even putting on any armour. His red eyes glared at his brother standing alone on the drawbridge.

"*You know that you can never defeat me,*" shouted Vaali. "*So go back or I'll be forced to beat you into the dust.*" He turned back.

"*Coward!*" yelled Sugreeva.

This was the last straw. Vaali uttered a savage war cry and rushed like a mad rhino at his brother. Their bodies clashed like two mountains in battle. Dust and rocks flew up around the two monkey warriors. From the bushes Raama could hardly make out one brother from the other. Vaali uprooted a huge tree and started to pound Sugreeva so hard on the head that Sugreeva began to yell for help and turned and escaped into the trees. Vaali stood still for a moment and then re-entered the palace.

Sugreeva was full of anger. Blood poured from the wounds on his head. He stormed over to Raama and said: "*You were supposed to kill him! What happened?*"

Raama shrugged. "*All I could see were two monkeys in the middle of a cloud of dust. I couldn't tell which one was Sugreeva and which one was Vaali.*"

Lakshmana had the answer. He made a garland of white flowers and wrapped it round Sugreeva's neck. "*That should help us know which one is you,*" he said. "*Are you ready to try again?*"

Sugreeva sat on a boulder to catch his breath while others washed his wounds in sweet smelling juices. He stood, took a deep breath and returned to the palace gate. "*Vaali!*" he shouted. "*Come out and fight for the crown you stole from me and the wife you stole from me. Come out you thief!*"

Inside the palace, Vaali heard his brother's cry and once

more exploded in anger. *"This time I will kill him,"* he roared.

The monkey queen, Taara, pleaded with him to stay. *"I feel that the signs are not good,"* she said. Vaali gently pushed her to one side and stormed out to meet his brother again.

QUEEN TAARA watched the fight from the top turrets of the palace. The two monkey brothers looked the size of water rats from the high window. Their bodies crashed into one another so hard that the drawbridge shuddered violently, throwing them both into the moat. They crawled out, gasping for breath, dripping with water. They proceeded to beat one another with their powerful fists and then with rocks and then with boulders. Sometimes Sugreeva was winning. Sometimes it was Vaali.

Then Vaali landed Sugreeva such a massive blow on the head that he reeled back and fell to the ground. Tearing a huge boulder from the ground, Vaali lifted it above his head and was about to smash it down on his brother ... Taara shut her eyes. A scream of pain that pierced the clouds and shook the window in its frame reached the heavens.

Taara opened her eyes. There was Sugreeva flat on the ground where he had fallen, but beside him, with an arrow in his back, lay the powerful Vaali.

"Vaali!" screamed Taara and she rushed down to the body of the dying ape. A crowd of monkeys and bears had formed a circle around the dying Vaali. Taara pushed and shoved her way through the bodies and came face to face with two tall handsome humans — one with a bow in his hand.

"Killer!" screamed Taara, pointing straight at Raama. *"How could you shoot a brave warrior like Vaali in the back?*

117

He wasn't even in battle with you. What kind of creature are you humans? Have you no honour? Have you no sense of right and wrong? Does killing give you pleasure?" The monkey queen, Taara, dropped to her knee, covered the bleeding body of Vaali with her veil and began to cry so sadly that some of the monkeys and bears turned away in shame.

Hanumaan lifted the weeping Taara to her feet, spoke quiet words of comfort and said: *"This is the mighty Raama, noble prince, great warrior, banished into the forest with his brother Lakshmana and wife Seeta on a black day over thirteen years ago. He is the enemy of the Dark Force and has made them so angry that one of the Night Rangers has stolen away his beautiful wife Seeta. Raama has come to us for help in getting her back."*

Taara laughed and then spat in the dust. *"That makes it worse,"* she hissed. *"How could a man who has lost his wife steal away my lord and master?"*

There was a long, long silence in which the buzz of a wasp one mile away could be heard. Then rising out of the silence came a feeble voice. It was Vaali. *"I have seen my death,"* he said. *"A place is being prepared for me in heaven. I am lucky to be killed by Raama's arrow, because all good creatures that are sent to death by Raama will surely find their place among the gods... So stop crying and be happy... Sugreeva... Sugreeva ... my anger has caused you a lot of hardship, forgive me... Take care of Taara and my son. Rule the kingdom wisely — I hope I have done the same..."* His eyes shut, and in the dying light, his body, red from the blood of a hundred wounds, shone like fields covered with rubies. With a long hiss, the last breath escaped from his body. Sugreeva carried Vaali's lifeless body into the palace grounds and shut the door.

The whole monkey kingdom was in mourning. Everyone loved the brave Vaali and the sound of wailing and crying melted the clouds and brought the rains. The rain poured for days and days without stop and soon the fields were like lakes and the streets of the city were like brown rivers of mud. And still the rain didn't stop. The lakes and rivers burst their banks and the hundred waterfalls on the mountains turned into thousands. The rain dragged out the smell of the earth. The rain washed away the blood from the battlefields. The rain meant that nobody moved from the monkey city and Raama and Lakshmana waited alone in a large dry cave in the mountainside.

Then the rain stopped and Raama was angry . . .

Abruptly Hanumaan stopped his story and left.

The search begins

AT LUNCHTIME THE NEXT DAY the children hardly touched their food.

"I don't know what's got into the two of you," said their mother. "For the last couple of days you have been restless and moody. What really happened at Aunt Sissey's?"

The boy told her how Aunt Sissey had burst into their secret playground in the poplars and had accused them of stealing her rugs and how, without thinking, he had thrown an orange at her.

"Whose rug was it, if it wasn't Aunt Sissey's?" asked their mother.

"Hanumaan's," said the boy.

"Whose?" said their mother.

The girl quickly said: "Actually we found it there when we first went to play. So we pretended it belonged to a person called Hanumaan."

"He's a monkey," said the boy. The girl kicked him under the table.

Their mother shook her head. "It is time you children learned that you can't live in a dream world."

The children nodded and sat without a word. And that's how Hanumaan found them later that day — sitting in their room without saying a word.

"Are we in a dream world?" asked the boy.

"How did you know about that part of the story?" said Hanumaan.

The two children jumped up. "Quickly, get to that part," they said.

"In time," said Hanumaan and the story continued . . .

RAAMA AND LAKSHMANA had waited patiently through the whole of the rainy season for Sugreeva to keep his promise and give them an army to search for Seeta. So when the rains finally stopped and there was still no word from Sugreeva, Raama became angry. He sent Lakshmana to the monkey king with a strong message.

Lakshmana found the court in a real mess — pillows scattered all around, monkeys swinging from the drapes, bears lying around drunk on honey wine. When he finally found Sugreeva, Lakshmana's eyes were burning with anger.

"King Sugreeva," he said, *"my brother Raama has sent me here to remind you of your promise to help him find the princess Seeta. Three months have passed and I find you in this place stupid with drink and power. If by tomorrow there is no action from you, we will storm down upon this kingdom with all our fury and reduce it to ashes!"*

Lakshmana's speech shocked Sugreeva. He looked around his court and saw that the words were true. Only one of his ministers wasn't drunk. It was Hanumaan who was sitting silently at a table eating nuts and oranges.

"Hanumaan," said Sugreeva, *"please use your gift of sweet words to calm Raama down."*

"Raama will not be happy with just sweet words," said Hanumaan.

"Yes, yes I know that," said Sugreeva. *"Tomorrow he will see action."*

Hanumaan bowed to the king and followed Lakshmana out of the court. Sugreeva clapped his hands and shouted: *"Send out the messengers, now! Every monkey in this kingdom is to assemble in the meadow-land outside the city before sunrise tomorrow."*

When Raama arrived the next morning he was greeted with a truly magnificent sight. The meadow and hills around the city were black with millions of monkeys and bears, all dressed for battle. The sky was filled with the sounds of trumpets and drums and commanders yelling orders and the neighing of horses and screams of elephants.

Sugreeva stood on the palace walls. *"Search every home, every cave, every forest and lake, every city and town in the whole land till you find the wife of our dear friend Raama. Be back with news within the month or face my fury. This is my command, so let it be done."*

Like a million ants crawling from an anthill, the army started to move out. Red Command went North, Blue Command went east, Green Command headed west and Yellow Command, led by Hanumaan and Vaali's son, headed south.

"I'm most impressed," said Raama. Then taking Lakshmana to one side he whispered: *"All reports have told us that the villain who stole Seeta headed south. Give this ring of mine to Hanumaan because I have a certain feeling that he will be successful in his search. If he finds Seeta, this will be his sign of friendship."*

ONE MONTH PASSED and the Red, Blue and Green army returned without any news. They had searched high and low, north, east and west and found nothing.

As the month was coming to an end the Yellow army, too, had had no success. They were exhausted and faint with hunger and thirst and were thinking about going back home. Then one of the bears came charging out of the trees. Panting heavily he said: *"There is a cave at the top of this mountain from which all sorts of wonderful birds are flying. We're bound to find fresh water in there."*

The cave looked cool and refreshing with mossy walls and

creepers hanging down. Two white cranes and a nightingale
flew out and the monkeys ducked because they were flying
so low. *"Follow me!"* said Vaali's son. The party of monkeys
and bears stepped into the darkness.

In the pitch black they could hardly see the ground and
the monkeys held onto one another as they entered deeper
and deeper, their ears picking up the roars of wild beasts,
their hair standing on end. Gradually the cave started to
become brighter and narrower. The monkeys were on hands
and knees, crawling through a low tunnel. Suddenly it
opened up and they found themselves in the most enchanting
land they had ever seen.

There were trees dripping with honey and blossoms and
jewels; houses of coral and diamonds; lakes of golden nectar;
and palaces with soft beds and silk clothes. The monkeys and
bears went crazy with enjoyment. They ate and drank and
lay on the soft beds and poured rubies over their heads and
yelled and charged around and went quite wild.

Only Hanumaan decided to explore further. Not far from
the golden city he came to a tiny hut and in it sat a very old
holy woman. Hanumaan bowed to her and said: *"Good lady,
we have come on a long journey and found this golden place by
chance. Tell us where we are."*

*"You have found the golden city built by the powerful Lord of
Illusion and Magic, the god Maya,"* she said, and then asked
Hanumaan to tell her their story. When she heard about
their mission to find Seeta she said: *"When you enter the cave
of Dreams Come True, time does funny things — a short time
seems like an age, and when you think no time has passed you have
wasted years in dream."*

"We've got to get out," said Hanumaan.

"No creature can escape from Maya's city on its own," said the old woman. *"But I will use my powers to help."*

All the monkeys gathered round, looking quite frightened. *"Shut your eyes,"* said the holy lady. They covered their eyes and then — in a magic flash — the next thing they heard was the sound of crashing waves and their noses stung with the smell of salt air. They were standing on the southernmost tip of the land, a huge ocean stretching before them.

It had only seemed like hours in the magical cave of Dreams Come True, but in fact weeks had passed. All their time had been used up. They had failed. Everyone was too frightened to return to face the fury of Sugreeva. So they decided to stay on the beach for ever.

TO CHEER THEMSELVES UP the monkeys on the beach began to tell stories. Hanumaan was the best storyteller and he started to tell of the adventures of Raama and Seeta. Little did he know that, watching from the darkness of the bushes, was an enormous old vulture — so old that he couldn't fly to catch his food any more. So when the vulture spied a huge gathering of plump and delicious looking monkeys and bears, he thanked the gods for sending him such a large feast. He licked his beak and started to creep up on them.

Just as the old vulture was about to pounce on the monkeys, Hanumaan reached the part in the story about how Jataayu had fought Raavana and had been killed by the King of the Night Rangers.

"Who speaks of Jataayu?" croaked the vulture. His voice gave the monkeys a fright.

Hanumaan jumped to his feet and stammered: *"I — I — I am Hanumaan, son of the Wind, chief minister of Sugreeva, friend of Raama whose wife was stolen by the Dark Force. Jataayu was trying to save her when he was killed. Who are you?"*

"I am the Vulture King, brother of Jataayu," said the ancient bird and he became sad at the news of his brother's death. Suddenly in a clear voice he said: *"I know where Seeta is."*

Everyone sat up straight. The Vulture King told them that he had seen Raavana's chariot flying southwards across the ocean and in it was a pale lady, white as the moon, her dress in shreds, her face stained with tears, headed straight towards the kingdom of Lanka.

The monkeys stared at the ocean which stretched for four hundred miles before them. How were they to get across?

Vaali's son turned to Hanumaan and said: *"I have heard tell of how, when you jump, you are like an eagle in flight. It's all down to you, Hanumaan. Jump."* And the others took up the chant: *"Jump! Jump! Jump!"*

HANUMAAN SHUT HIS EYES and his body started to grow larger and larger, till he was the size of a towering mountain. He looked around for something he could spring off and found a fern-covered hill that would do the job perfectly. He placed his right foot on the hill and tested its strength. It was firm.

Then, coiling all his muscles, he pressed back with his foot so hard that the hill was squeezed and snakes and foxes burst out of the ground and water hissed out of underground streams and seams of precious metals melted and poured out of cracks. The mountain was glistening and hissing and groaning and steaming.

Then everything settled down. The ground became rock hard. Hanumaan was ready.

He steadied his senses, sniffed at the wind, gathered all his force, his hair standing on end, his ears flapped back, his breath controlled.

Then shouting: *"Victory to Raama!"* he leapt.

High, high, high he floated, the wind carrying him at the speed of a comet flashing through the night sky. Suddenly a huge mountain shot up from the sea, blocking his path, but he kicked it to dust.

"I was only trying to give you a place for rest," said the mountain.

"I'm sorry, but there's no need for rest," said Hanumaan and he floated higher and faster like the wind.

Then, suddenly, there came a roar from the depths of the ocean and the sea swirled round in massive whirlpools. A dark shape shot to the surface and burst through the waves.

It was a massive sea serpent with enormous claws and teeth, jaws wide open. Hanumaan's body grew and grew and the monster's mouth opened wider and wider. Then suddenly Hanumaan shrunk down to the size of a fly and flew straight through the monster.

His friends on the sea shore cheered him on. The gods in the heavens cheered him on. And Hanumaan, strengthened by thoughts of Raama, crossed the mighty ocean and landed safely in Lanka, kingdom of the Night Rangers, home of the Dark Force.

"You were the hero!" cried the girl.

"It was a truly wonderful evening," said Hanumaan. "And my father, the Wind, did help a lot. At one moment, when I was running out of steam and I felt myself dropping closer and closer to the waves, a gust of wind gently picked me up and carried me high into the clouds and I surfed on the high currents of air all the way to Lanka. You should try it sometime."

"I bet Lanka was smelly and slimy and black," said the boy.

"Quite the reverse," said Hanumaan. "It was magnificent. But enough for now. Do you realise that we have begun our last few stories. Things definitely take a turn from here on."

"We can't wait any longer," said the boy.

"The ending has already started, silly," said the girl. "Hasn't it, Hanumaan?"

But Hanumaan had disappeared.

A full moon filled the night sky. And then the boy saw it — the tiny figure of Hanumaan flying across the face of the moon.

Day 16
Hanumaan finds Seeta

ALTHOUGH THE END for the evil Raavana was in sight, the children discovered that all was not really well. There was a restlessness in their hearts ever since the story of Seeta's kidnapping. And it wasn't just them.

At home, too, things were a bit edgy. They heard their parents talking the night before about how things seemed to be going wrong at their father's work. "I don't know what's going on," he said. "Every time I seem to be getting on top of things, some disaster hits and I'm back on the ground again. What is going on?"

The bad news seemed to make their mother tired and, at breakfast that morning, the girl found her at the table with eyes red from tears. Quickly her mother stood up and dried her nose on her apron and said: "It's nothing, dear, it's just that I need a holiday."

So another morning passed in boredom and restlessness and quarrels. "What is happening to us?" said the girl.

"You mean, what's happening to you?" said the boy. And another quarrel started. By tea time, when Hanumaan arrived, the children were not even talking to one another.

"Maybe I should come back another time," said Hanumaan and he rose to leave. But both children grabbed him by his arms and pulled him down again. He looked at their faces with his wise eyes full of affection. "The sadness will pass," he said. "Life may serve up bitter food, but ..." he paused, looking from one face to the other, "... there are always oranges!" And he whipped out two huge oranges from his shoulder pouch.

The children burst into smiles. "Ahh, where's the sadness now?" said Hanumaan. "Things can't be that serious if all it takes to shift matters is an orange."

The girl gave him a hug. "You're a trickster," she said.

"Tell us about Lanka," said the boy. They all settled down.

Hanumaan's eyes took on a far away look. "Yes," he said, "I was telling you about Hanumaan's magnificent jump to Lanka . . ."

AFTER HIS FEET HIT THE GROUND, Hanumaan dusted down his fur and shrunk himself down to the size of an ordinary little monkey. This was the best way to move about un-noticed in the city. He left behind the sea and green fields and soon found himself outside the walls of Lanka. There were guards all over the place, all armed to the teeth with dangerous looking weapons. But no one paid any attention to a tiny monkey who quietly slipped past into the city.

The beauty of the place took Hanumaan's breath away. Tall buildings, broad streets and beautiful people. Hanumaan had thought that it wouldn't be difficult to spot Seeta because she would be the only beauty in a place of ugliness. But here he saw beauty everywhere: in the trees, the women, the fountains, the laughing children, the fluttering flags, the musicians and jugglers, the markets and temples.

And there, towering above the whole city was Raavana's palace. High turrets touched the clouds. Walls of gold, festooned with multi-coloured flags and banners, flashed in the sunlight, equalling the home of the king of the gods.

"This is where he's taken Seeta," thought Hanumaan, heading towards the palace walls. But suddenly the earth split and a tall and powerful lady shot out to block his path.

"I am Lanka, Guardian Spirit of this city. No stranger enters here," she said and gave Hanumaan a heavy blow on his chest knocking him to the ground. Quick as a flash he was back on his feet and, before he could stop himself, gave

Lanka a slap on her face, knocking her to the ground. He stiffened himself for a fight.

But, much to his surprise the lady knelt before him and touched his feet. *"I know who you are, my Lord,"* she said. *"The ancient story goes that when Lanka is slapped on the face by a monkey, the city will be destroyed. Please enter the palace. I will not try to stop you."*

Hanumaan did not need a second invitation. In the twinkling of an eye, he scaled the high walls and dropped down to the cool grass of the palace gardens. They were truly magnificent gardens, bursting with flowers of every sort, dotted with lawns where ladies played with hoops, their laughing voices like tinkling bells, their movements as graceful as autumn cranes.

EVERYWHERE HANUMAAN LOOKED he saw beautiful women. They were in the bedrooms of the palace, lying like swans on silken sheets, smiling in their sleep. Or they were singing sweet love songs to the soldiers. Their faces were lit by jewels, their eyes were the shape of almonds, their necks slender like gazelles, their hips swayed like the sails of ships billowing in the gentle evening breeze as they moved, their tiny feet were decorated with ankle bells that made chink, chink sounds as they walked.

But Hanumaan could not see Seeta. Room after room he searched with no luck. Finally he came to Raavana's inner chamber. There was the Lord of the Dark Force himself, lying drinking wine on soft cushions, a most magnificent figure, surrounded by even more beautiful ladies. There was one among them who was so beautiful that Hanumaan was certain that he had found Seeta. She stood apart from the others, looking out of the window with a slightly sad look in her sparkling green eyes.

Hanumaan gave a little shudder. *"What am I thinking?"* he said to himself, *"Seeta would never, never be here. Search somewhere else!"* Hanumaan swung out of the window and down the creeper that clung to the castle wall and was back in the city again. He searched all over till the sun turned into a flaming red ball and settled low in the sky, bathing the whole of Lanka in its red light. Hanumaan became sad. *"I have failed Raama,"* he said. *"Seeta is nowhere to be found."*

THEN, JUST AS HE TURNED BACK to the sea, he spotted a tiny walled garden on a hill in the distance. It was one place that he hadn't visited. There was something about it, however, that made his hair stand on end: it was shining with a magical white glow. Hanumaan leapt and ran and skipped and bounded and was soon below the walls of the garden. The sign above the golden gate read: *Ashoka Garden.*

With one leap, Hanumaan was over the wall and, swinging from tree to tree, searching the grounds at high speed. The smell of blossoms filled his heart with happiness, the colour of the flowers dazzled his eyes.

And then he saw her . . .

Right in the centre of the Ashoka Garden was a tiny pavilion made of white marble. And right in the middle of the pavilion was a white marble bench. And sitting on the bench was the figure of a woman, her head bowed, her eyes streaming with tears, her clothes torn and stained, her hair undone, coiling like a hundred black snakes down her back and shoulders.

She lifted her white face and cried: *"Raama, Raama, how could you have forgotten me? Why do you leave me here?"*

Hanumaan knew that his search had ended. But before he could present himself to the lady Seeta, hordes of the most horrible she-demons chased her into the bushes. *"Now you little toad,"* one shrieked, *"how many times have we told you to stop that wailing!"* She gave Seeta a shove with her scaly green hand.

The others held her back. *"If Raavana finds out that you touched her, all of us will be lion's meat."*

"But I've had enough of her!" screamed the green hag. *"All she does all day is sit and cry and sigh and snivel and say: Raama! Raama! That word hurts my ears."*

Seeta turned on the hag, her eyes red with anger and tears. *"When Raama comes to get me, it will be more than your ears that hurt."*

"Ooo, look at the angry little miss!" taunted a one-eyed hag.

"You look beautiful when you're angry, dearie," hissed another, who had a nose which was permanently running with green stuff. And they all laughed and teased and taunted and mocked. They were truly a sight from hell. Seeta just shut her eyes. Hanumaan stayed hidden in the tree.

AT SUNRISE THE NEXT DAY the ugly hags were sound asleep. Seeta tiptoed to the sparkling water fountain and washed her face. Her left eye began to twitch. *"It's an omen that something good is about to happen,"* she thought. A tiny fawn peeped out of the bushes and Seeta held out a handful of grass. With nervous footsteps the fawn edged towards her, sniffed at the grass and began to eat. Seeta nuzzled the fawn's neck with her nose.

This was the moment that Hanumaan was waiting for.

He jumped from the tree. Seeta gave a sharp little cry and the hag without a nose started to wake. "*Ssh!*" said Hanumaan. He whispered: "*I have come to you from Raama.*"

Seeta shook her head. "*No. This is another trick.*"

Hanumaan stretched out his hand and there shining in his long black palm was Raama's ring. Seeta gasped and put her hands to her mouth.

"*Follow me! Now! For Raama's sake,*" said Hanumaan and Seeta followed him to a green lawn away from the snoring hags. There Hanumaan told her of everything that had happened since she had been kidnapped. Seeta cried when she heard that the mighty vulture Jataayu was dead. Her eyes lit up when she heard of his friendship with the monkey king Sugreeva. And she gave a merry clap when she heard of Hanumaan's leap across the ocean.

"*Good lady, I am strong enough to save you myself. These Night Rangers are no match for me. But I think it would be only proper if Raama himself comes here and destroys the wretch who stole you away,*" said Hanumaan. "*So be patient a little longer and we will be back with an army so powerful that even the demons in hell will tremble with fear.*"

"*Then go quickly, brother Hanumaan,*" said Seeta. She removed her earrings and handed them to Hanumaan. "*Give these to Raama. Maybe they will make him get here sooner.*" And Seeta broke into sobs that sounded so sad that Hanumaan wanted to do something terrible to punish those who had made her life such a nightmare.

"*I'll destroy them. I'll reduce them to ashes. I'll flatten their fancy houses and rip up their golden streets. They will know then what fear is!*"

Hanumaan stopped speaking. His voice was coming in short bursts. His hair was standing on end, ears flattened back, lips curling to show pink gums and sharp yellow teeth.

"I am angry even now," he said. "Raavana definitely made a mistake when he stole Seeta. When I think of that good lady surrounded by those wretched hags my blood runs through my veins like molten lava, waiting to explode. I must stop now."

Abruptly Hanumaan rose, and left.

Day 17
Hanumaan on fire

THE GIRL WATCHED HER FATHER getting ready for work the next morning. All his movements were steady and beautiful. She loved watching him shave, first whipping up a lather in the soap bowl with his favourite brush and plenty of hot water. The brush deftly covered his jaw with lather, leaving just his lips standing out pink from the white foam.

Each movement of the blade left a clean path through the white lather. She couldn't help imitating the way he pulled faces so that the razor got into every corner. "What are you staring at, monkey?" he laughed.

"Your funny face," she said. And he grabbed her and wiped a blob of lather onto her nose. "Now who looks like a clown?" he said.

She followed him into the bedroom and watched him pull on his white shirt. "Are things bad at work?" she asked.

"Not really," he said. "And even if they were, your father would still dress and go in."

She handed him his favourite red cuff-links. Then, before she had time to stop the words, she heard herself say: "You remind me of Raama preparing for battle."

Her father stopped. "I didn't realise you knew the story," he said.

"I didn't know you did," she beamed.

He tapped her nose: "So, little madam, it seems as if you don't know everything after all."

The girl was thinking about this strange talk much later in the day when Hanumaan burst in like a storm.

"My Dad has heard of Raama," said the girl.

"I know," said Hanumaan sharply. "But we'll speak about that later. Lanka must be destroyed first." The children sat still. Hanumaan shut his eyes and the story gently filled the room . . .

ANGER BURNS LIKE FIRE. And when Hanumaan
remembered the sadness of Seeta, surrounded as she was by
the most ugly of she-demons, he became angry. He grew his
body to an enormous size, raised his head to the rising sun
and ROARED. This spread confusion among the hags in the
Ashoka Gardens. They jumped to their feet, still half asleep,
and ran hither and thither like chickens who have seen the
fox. One of them spotted Hanumaan and, uttering a horrible
scream, charged at him. He swatted her like a cow's tail
swats flies. She rolled dead in the dust.

Then Hanumaan leapt down to the pavilion and tore out
one of its marble pillars. The whole place crumbled to the
ground. He swung the pillar round and round like a club
and pounded the she-demons to dust. One of them managed
to get away and she ran as fast as she could to the palace
where everyone had been woken by Hanumaan's roar.

News that a monster was destroying the city reached
Raavana. In his fury he said: *"Why do I have to be disturbed
by tales of a monkey? Surely someone else can get rid of that pest."*

Raavana's youngest son, a brave and sturdy lad, begged his
father to let him go to kill the monkey. Raavana agreed and
made sure that his son had a fine chariot with thousands of
arrows and spears and watched as he galloped through the
palace gates, raising a cloud of dust behind him.

Hanumaan, too, watched the chariot get nearer. He smiled
when he saw the handsome prince, shining in his new
armour like a god in battle. Then just as he thought that it
was a pity to destroy such a fine young fellow, a cloud of
arrows from the chariot swarmed down on Hanumaan,
stinging his body and face and arms.

He collected his strength, charged towards the prince and

a mighty fight took place. The brave lad was fast and his arrows kept showering down on Hanumaan, but the monkey fought like a raging hurricane and soon the prince was dead. Hanumaan raised his voice to heaven and cried: *"Victory to Raama!"*

Hanumaan's voice carried the sound of Raama's name deep into the palace, spreading terror. It was a name that Raavana feared; it was a name that was constantly on his mind; it was a name that made him wake at night; it was a name that sometimes made his heart still. *"I myself will put an end to this matter,"* he said, calling for his armour.

But the doors burst open and in strode a magnificent warrior, Indrajit, Raavana's most powerful son. He bowed before his father and then with a voice as cold as steel he said: *"Let me send this wretched ape to the kingdom of death."*

Indrajit's skill as a warrior was well known. In fact he had even defeated the king of the gods in battle and had won all the god's magic weapons. There was no one in Lanka who was his equal in battle. So Raavana agreed to let his second son fight. *"Do not kill him,"* said Raavana, *"but use your Serpent Arrow to snare him and bring him bound to me."*

Indrajit bowed, climbed into his chariot drawn by lions and soon reached the Ashoka Gardens.

Hanumaan's eyes lit up with delight at the skill of the young warrior he faced. Indrajit's arrows brought Hanumaan down to the ground, but soon the mighty monkey was on his feet again. He tore up a huge oak tree from the garden and smashed down Indrajit's lions. The prince rolled in the dust and was up again, arrows sparking from his golden bow. But Hanumaan, that bull among monkeys, rained down blows so fast and furious that the prince feared that he was about to meet his first defeat.

Then, finally drawing his Serpent Arrow from the quiver, Indrajit shot it straight towards Hanumaan. The arrow hit Hanumaan's body with a hiss, coiling round him and bringing him to the ground. Hanumaan was bound. A cheer went up from the Night Rangers and they danced around Hanumaan's body with clubs and spears and beat him and taunted him. Blood poured from Hanumaan's wounds, making him look like a splendid lake at sunset. He let out a ferocious roar and the demons jumped back in fear.

"Bring rope and vine to tie him," they yelled. But Indrajit, knowing that rope and vine would break the magic of the Serpent Arrow, shouted: *"NO!"* Too late — the others had wrapped Hanumaan from head to toe with stout ropes and vines. Hanumaan knew that he was free, but he pretended that he was bound and let the Night Rangers drag him to Raavana's palace.

"Who are you?" roared Raavana.

"I am destruction to your city and death to you. I carry words of terror to Lanka from the magnificent lord Raama whose wife you have stolen in the most cowardly way. Too frightened to face the noble Raama in a square fight, you sneaked in like a beggar when his back was turned."

Hanumaan's words stung Raavana deeply. Grabbing a sword Raavana rushed towards the bound monkey, ready to cut off his head. But he was stopped in his action by a calm voice from the back of the court: *"It is not proper for a king to kill a messenger."* The crowd parted and there stood Raavana's good brother, Vibeeshana.

Raavana was returned to his senses by his brother's words.

"Take this creature from my sight and punish him for killing my youngest son," he said. *"Take him into the public square and set his tail alight."*

THE SOLDIERS DRAGGED HANUMAAN into the city, followed by a jeering crowd. They wrapped his tail in rags soaked in grease and oil and set it alight. Hanumaan had seen all that he wanted to and had now had enough. He burst free of his bonds and, growing to the height of a mountain, he thumped his fiery tail on the ground, sending an earthquake through the city, destroying hundreds of buildings. In his anger he swished his mighty tail setting fire to anything that was left standing.

The city of Lanka in flames was like a picture of hell, men and women rushing around screaming in terror and pain. Hanumaan leapt from this flaming city and landed once more in the Ashoka Gardens. *"This place which has been the prison of gentle Seeta cannot escape my fury."* Then, like a mighty hurricane, Hanumaan tore up trees and flowers and bushes, smashed down the walls and set fire to what was left.

Suddenly he stopped in horror. *"Seeta!"* he cried. *"In the blindness of my anger I have killed Seeta!"* He rushed like a mad thing through the flames of the Ashoka Gardens and there saw Seeta, still sitting on the lawn where they had met, perfectly safe. The God of Fire had drawn a magic circle around the weeping princess and kept her from harm.

"Hanumaan, save me!" cried Seeta.

"Have courage," said Hanumaan. *"I will be back soon with a mighty army led by Raama and Lakshmana."* Saying that, Hanumaan leapt on to a small mountain overlooking the sea and prepared for his flight back home. He shut his eyes,

drew together all his strength, and shouting *"Honour to Seeta!"* launched himself on to the wind. The ocean threw up a mist of spray to cool the wounded monkey and put out the flames on his tail. From high above the clouds he could see the vast blue ocean with the island of Lanka like a flaming red broach on her breast.

THERE WAS GREAT CELEBRATION when Hanumaan landed among his friends. They had a million questions and could hardly hide their glee when they heard the tales of his adventure. They went wild with joy, lifting Hanumaan on to their shoulders and carrying him all the way back home.

When news of their return reached Raama, he was with them in a flash. *"They wouldn't be celebrating if they had failed,"* he said to Lakshmana. *"Hanumaan has found Seeta."*

Hanumaan bowed before the two princes. *"Victory is ours,"* he said. *"The princess Seeta is safe and she sends you her tender love. She will be counting the days till she is face to face with her Lord once more."*

"How can you be sure it was Seeta?" asked Lakshmana.

Hanumaan held out the earrings given to him by Seeta. Raama took them gently from his hand and his heart swelled with hope. He walked into the cool woods with Hanumaan and they talked about Seeta and made plans for battle.

"Tomorrow we must leave for Lanka," said Raama.

His word was law.

The children were listening open mouthed now. Hanumaan clapped and they blinked into the present. "I want you to see something," said Hanumaan. "Leave quietly and peep into the kitchen."

Voices came from the kitchen. "Dad's home," whispered the boy.

"Ssh, listen," said the girl. Silently they peeped through the open door and saw their mother with a single red rose in her hands.

"It's beautiful," she was whispering. "Thank you."

Their father gave her a kiss on the cheek. "The beauty is not the rose," he said. "The rose can only be beautiful because your mind is beautiful, because your heart is beautiful, because you are beautiful deep down. Thank you."

The girl drew the door shut and they tiptoed upstairs. Hanumaan had gone.

Day 18
Raama in Lanka

WHEN HANUMAAN RETURNED the next day, there was something different about him. He unwrapped a little bundle he had brought and in it were two oranges and a few nuts. He offered them to the children without a word and climbed on to the bed, ready to continue his story.

"Is something wrong?" asked the boy.

"It's always best to be quiet on the eve of battle," Hanumaan smiled.

"But it's only a battle in the story," said the boy.

"The war against the Lord of Dark Force is never won by a single battle..." said Hanumaan.

"But surely..." began the boy. His sister stopped him speaking another word. She said: "Listen to his voice!"

And, as they listened, the hairs on the back of their necks started to tingle because the voice they heard coming from Hanumaan's lips was exactly like their father's...

THE DAY HAD COME for Sugreeva's army to make their journey southward to save Seeta. By noon the hills and forests, meadows and fields were covered with soldiers. The gods in the heavens showered rose petals on the huge army of monkeys and bears. Queen Taara and the wives of the soldiers each arrived carrying a white bird. And at the very second of noon they set the birds free: the sky filled with the hum of flapping wings and the brightness of thousands of white birds.

Battle orders went out. With a blare of trumpets and a boom of drums the army of Sugreeva started the march on Lanka. The fastest soldiers led the march. Raama,

Lakshmana, Hanumaan, Sugreeva and Vaali's son were in the middle and the powerful bull apes and bears followed up at the rear. Spies were sent ahead to make sure that there were no traps set by the Night Rangers. Special troops were assigned to hunt for food. Others had the job of setting up camp in safe places. Raama's order was that no village or town was to be damaged by the army and the rice fields were to remain untouched. It was a massive operation.

All the soldiers were certain of victory. Raama could hear them talking. Some boasted that they had the strength to kill Raavana on their own. Others said that they would tear down what was left of Lanka with bare hands. Others said that they would trample every Night Ranger into the dust with one foot. But then there were those who marched in silence, their minds steady, their hearts pure. They neither drank too much nor ate too much. Each sunset they would gather their strength in rest and prayer.

They marched miles and miles, resting beside lakes of pure water, sleeping in forests rich with fruit and flowers, crossing mighty rivers and deep ravines. By the time they finally reached the sea, there was just one obstacle left: how was such a huge army going to cross the sea?

THAT NIGHT Raama stood on the cliffs and looked out over the ocean. It was as black as ink. Clouds scudded across the face of the moon. The late gulls practised their diving and then hurried home. Waves like mountains pounded the rocks with thunderous force and the mighty ocean swelled and sank like a breathing, living monster at sleep.

Down below were the tiny campfires of the army. The lazy night air carried up the sounds of the camp: soldiers telling stories and laughing, the crackle of fire and cooking, the soft sounds of pots and pans being washed while snuffling horses beat their hooves on the black rocks of the shore. It all seemed so happy down there. And Raama began to feel sad again. For when Seeta had been stolen from him, he had lost his peace.

In his mind he saw her as Hanumaan had described her, surrounded by ugly hags, mocked, teased, tormented. Then he remembered her at the happier times in the forest, chasing dragonflies, picking berries, swimming in lotus pools and laughing her laugh that lit up the darkest corners of people's hearts. Raama felt the beating of his heart. *"O brave lady, soon you will be by my side again. Have courage. It won't be long now."*

FOUR THOUSAND MILES south of where Raama stood was another solitary figure. Raavana, too, had thoughts of war. His spies had brought news of the march of the monkey army and the bravery of Raama. They told of the strength of the bears. They told of how high the monkeys could leap and how powerful were the fists of the bull apes. They spoke of the glory of Raama and the speed of his brother Lakshmana.

Still Raavana did not want to give up Seeta. He was mad in his love for her. He could not bear the thought of losing her. She had brought peace even to him in his evil kingdom. *"There is no turning back now,"* he said. *"These men have killed my brothers and my uncle. They mocked my sister and cruelly cut off her nose. They must die."*

All Raavana's generals told him that there was nothing to

fear and they boasted about their victories and strength. *"If I get my hands on Raama,"* said one of them, *"I'll tear his body to shreds and drink his blood."*

"Ah, but remember that Raama is the man who managed to kill fourteen thousand of our best troops single handed," said a calm voice from the crowd. It was Raavana's good brother, Vibeeshana. He told Raavana that it was wrong to steal another man's wife and that he should stop the war. But the generals called him a coward and laughed at him.

"You are all too quick to choose war," said Vibeeshana. *"We haven't tried to speak to Raama first and stop this terrible war."*

Raavana roared in fury: *"You speak like a sheep, not the brother of the most powerful Lord of the Dark Force. Even the gods fear me because they can't kill me. I have shot my arrows at Death and seen him run away. Why should I fear a puny man?"*

"Because you are wrong!" said his brother. *"I will not stay here any longer and be part of your evil."* He turned and left the court.

USING HIS MAGIC POWERS, Vibeeshana lifted like a comet into the night, flew across the ocean through a sky studded with stars and landed at sunrise right in the middle of the monkey army. His landing caused great commotion. Monkeys and bears rushed all over the place looking for their weapons. *"The battle has started,"* they shouted.

Finally, fifty monkeys pounced upon Raavana's brother, bound him with thick ropes and dragged him to Raama.

"I have come in peace," said the Night Ranger.

"He's a spy," shouted the generals. *"He's Raavana's brother."*

"I come to build the peace," he said.

And Raama knew from the sound of his voice that he was

the good side of the Dark Force. *"Untie him,"* said Raama. *"Gentle sir, when your brother stole my wife, he called death down upon his family. Stay with us and, when we have destroyed Raavana and all his evil followers, you will be crowned king of Lanka."* Then, turning to Sugreeva, Raama said: *"I want this waiting to end now."*

"But Raama, the ocean is a tough enemy," said Sugreeva.

"Then the ocean needs to be taught a lesson," said Raama and, grabbing his bow, he stormed over to the ocean's edge followed by hundreds of monkeys.

Raama stood on a black boulder and shouted to the sea: *"Are you going to let us across? Or do you have to be forced by me to yield?"*

The waves kept rolling and crashing with angry foam against the rocks. Then Raama shouted: *"YIELD!"* and fired such powerful arrows into the ocean that the water turned to steam, fish and whales rose up and begged him to stop and the monkeys thought that he was going to make the ocean into a desert.

Finally, the God of the Sea himself rose like a mountainous wave from the ocean depths and said: *"Stop, Raama. Do not ask me to act against my nature. I am the sea and the sea does not part for an army of monkeys. But if you want to cross, throw down boulders into the waves and the ocean will help you build a giant causeway to Lanka."*

ALL NIGHT LONG the army of monkeys and bears tore huge rocks from the mountainside and threw them into the waves. The chief monkey builder, who had built the kingdom of the gods, gave the orders: *"We want more small rocks here."* *"Start filling in the cracks with moss and soft*

grasses." "I don't want any more red stones — bring me round black ones."

Hour after hour the work continued. Monkeys were dropping from tiredness. In the end even Raama and Lakshmana, Sugreeva and Hanumaan joined the workers. Their skill and speed inspired the monkeys and bears whose strength returned once more.

By the time the sun rose the next day, the beautiful causeway was complete. It was broad and steady, made with black boulders decorated with red rock and softened by mosses and sweet smelling grasses. Raama and the chief monkey builder walked its whole length, checking details, patting in the moss here, removing sharp rocks there.

Raama was satisfied. He shot a flaming arrow into the sky. This was the signal to advance. The huge army started to march to Lanka . . .

Hanumaan stepped off the bed. "Tomorrow the battle will start for real," he said. "I need to be prepared." He walked over to the girl's desk and picked up her family photo album. Slowly he flicked through the images, from babies to holidays to funny faces and friends. He stopped at the picture of her father — the one she loved most. He studied it for a long while in silence.

Finally, drawing it out of its album sleeve, he carefully wedged it in the mirror frame. The children watched in silence, their eyes widening at what was happening before them . . .

Hanumaan's reflection in the mirror started to become transparent and then solid and transparent again and solid once more. And, from time to time, instead of Hanumaan's face reappearing, they saw the face of their father. "We're ready," said Hanumaan.

He turned to the children and gave them each a hug, filling them with light. "Don't expect anything tomorrow," he said. "Don't reject anything. Just be still and calmly face whatever meets you."

"I don't know if I like the sound of this," said the boy. "Are we in a trouble again?"

Hanumaan smiled. "Quite the reverse," he said. "I must disappear now; but I'll never be far."

A strong wind filled the room, flapping the curtains like huge trapped birds. By the time the girl managed to shut the window, Hanumaan had vanished. It was a strange moment. The girl felt a sadness in her heart that was very, very deep and yet she found herself quite calm. "I doubt if we'll be seeing Hanumaan again," she said.

Day 19
War begins

TIME DRAGGED the next day. Each time the breeze stirred, the children expected to see Hanumaan, but it was only a branch or loose paper or clothes on the line. Evening came and still no sign of the friendly monkey, the son of the Wind God.

The girl was up in her room, clearing away the mess of papers on her desk, when she heard the sound of a key in the front door and ran downstairs. Their father was back. He took off his jacket and shouted up to his son to run a bath. He handed his daughter a carrier bag. "Put these in a bowl," he said.

They were oranges — bright and plump with juice. There were nuts too. The girl wiped each orange till it shone Then she placed the fruit in a flat wooden bowl. She knew what she had to do next. She cleared a space in the living room and placed a rug neatly in the middle, arranged with candles, nuts and the bowl of beautiful oranges. The boy helped her.

Their father came down from his bath looking refreshed. "This looks nice," he said looking round the room. "What's it in aid of?"

The girl took his hand and led him to the centre of the room. "Today you are going to tell us the rest of Hanumaan's story."

"Am I?" said their father, and his eyes sparkled with thoughts of his own childhood. "Very well," he said, "where would you like me to start?"

The boy looked at his sister whose eyes hadn't left her father's. "Would you tell us about the battle," he said.

His father nodded. "I think I can remember that ..."

THEIR MARCH ACROSS THE GIANT CAUSEWAY had taken the monkey army the best part of the day. Dusk was falling when they finally reached the island kingdom of

Lanka. It was still an impressive sight, despite the
destruction wrought by the fire. Signs of preparation for
battle could be seen. Clusters of soldiers were rushing here
and there to take up their positions. The sound of trumpets
and drums could be heard and the occasional cry of a war
elephant.

The monkey army, too, was keen to start. They practised
their giant leaps, some jumping clear over the tall trees on
the mountain. The bears displayed their enormous strength,
tearing huge boulders from the mountainside and tossing
them in the air as if they were juggling balls. Raama,
Lakshmana, Sugreeva and Hanumaan climbed to the top of a
high mountain and looked down at the city.

Hanumaan pointed out the palace and suddenly, there
on the ramparts, appeared the figure of Raavana. Sugreeva
let out a whoop of excitement and, before anyone could
stop him, he charged down the mountain and leapt over
the walls of the city. He scaled the palace gates at top speed
and stood proudly before Raavana. *"Meet your doom,"* he
cried and hurled himself at the powerful Lord of the Dark
Force.

Raavana was taken by surprise and was knocked to the
ground. A huge cheer went up from the monkey army. But
Raavana was soon on his feet again. He grabbed Sugreeva by
the waist in an iron grip. The two were equally matched in
wrestling. In the end Sugreeva began to tire. Uttering
another loud whoop he leapt away and was back on the
mountain once more. Monkeys and bears all applauded and
cried: *"Sugreeva! Sugreeva!"* But Raama's face was dark.

"Never pull a stunt like that again," he said, his voice cold
and steady. Sugreeva filled with shame and looked to the

ground. *"You are a king,"* said Raama. *"I need you to lead your army, not take stupid risks at this very important time when we need our reason steady. This war will be conducted according to proper rules. Send a messenger to Raavana and tell him that he has no hope of victory. For the good of his subjects, tell him to surrender Seeta to me and avoid the terrible waste that will surely follow if he refuses."*

Vaali's son carried the message. He showed no fear as he stood before the magnificent warriors. He delivered his message clearly and slowly. Raavana admired the courage of the young ape. He listened to every word.

"If you are finished," he said, *"hear my words."* He clapped twice.

Two guards were at his side in a flash. *"Kill this messenger,"* he said.

The guards hesitated for a moment because it was wrong to kill a messenger. This was all the time that Vaali's brave son needed. He grabbed the guards, one under each of his powerful arms, and leapt high into the sky, kicking the turret of the palace to pieces as he flew.

Once more a cheer went up from the monkey army and fear began to spread among the Night Rangers because they saw the broken turret as a bad sign.

Raavana sent out spies disguised as monkeys into Raama's camp that night, but they were easily spotted by Raavana's good brother Vibeeshana, who knew all the tricks of the Night Rangers and their ways of magic. Soldiers captured the spies and brought them before Raama.

"What should we do with these villains?" they asked.

"Release them," said Raama. *"Take them around the camp, show them everything. Then, when they are trembling with fear*

at the smell of death, let them return to their squalid little army."
And that's just what happened.

The spies returned to Raavana's court quaking with fear.
*"Raama looks as fierce as the God of Death. His constant
companion and brother, Lakshmana, burns with anger. Then there
are the powerful leaders of the monkeys, Sugreeva, Hanumaan and
the brave Vaali's son. We saw a huge army of bears uprooting
trees and tearing massive boulders from the mountainside in
preparation for battle. We fear for our people. Give up this
terrible sin of yours. Let Seeta free."*

"Never!" roared Raavana. *"I, who even the gods fear, will
never surrender to that puny mortal. Tomorrow we fight."*

EARLY THE NEXT MORNING the gates to Lanka
crashed open and, uttering blood-curdling cries, the army of
Night Rangers poured out like black lava from a volcano.
Trumpets were sounded in Raama's camp and the monkey
army swarmed down the mountain to meet their enemy.

The clash was terrible. The sounds of war were
frightening. The sights made even brave warriors pale with
horror. Arms and legs and heads were smashed. Rocks and
trees crashed down on the Night Rangers. Thousands of
monkeys were brought to the ground by arrows and spears,
maces and clubs.

Raama's bow was never idle. It smoked with heat as flights
of arrows of every sort spread death and confusion wherever
they landed. The Night Rangers scattered in fear when they
saw him approach. And never far behind was Lakshmana,
sowing terror with his bravery.

Night fell, but the army of the Dark Force continued to
fight. Fires had sprung up through the city. The wails of

women were carried on the still black air like so many ghosts. They pierced the heavens, they entered the Ashoka Garden where Seeta prayed for the safety of her Lord, they shook the beautiful statues in the golden palace of Raavana.

The Lord of the Dark Force covered his ears against the screams of death. *"Why is this taking so long?"* he yelled.

"Father, let me loose on this army of ignorant monkeys and I will put an end to this war," said Indrajit, Raavana's eldest son.

"Do what must be done," snapped Raavana.

Indrajit was in his chariot in no time and soon entered the thick of battle, crushing thousands of monkeys and bears under his massive wheels. Nothing could stop this valiant warrior. He had one target in mind and he headed straight for it — Raama! The monkey generals tried to form a ring to protect Raama, but one by one they fell under Indrajit's weapons. Sugreeva leapt onto Indrajit's chariot and grabbed the young warrior around his throat, but he too was swatted off as if he was a harmless mosquito.

Finally, Indrajit got a clear view of Raama and Lakshmana fighting back to back against the swarms of Night Rangers that flew towards them like moths into a fire. Indrajit drew two Serpent Darts from his quiver, aimed and let fly. Hissing their poisonous death, the arrows sped surely towards the princes of Ayodhya. Raama and Lakshmana fell to the ground like chopped trees.

A huge cheer went up in the Night Ranger camp. Raavana's proud warrior son rushed to the palace with news of Raama's death. People shook his hand and clapped him on the back. Raavana put his arms around his son's shoulders and showed him proudly to the assembled generals.

"Now this is what I call a warrior," he said. *"Well done, my son."*

One of the scaly green spies pushed his way to the front of the crowd, trailing slime in his wake. *"If your Lord pleases to hear me, I would say: show Seeta that her husband is dead and she will fall into your arms. And victory will be ours."* He sniffed and wiped his nose.

"Good idea," said Raavana.

Soon a golden chariot drawn by swans carried Seeta high above the battlefield. The good lady uttered a cry and covered her face at what she saw. There, in the middle of the field of blood, lay the motionless bodies of Raama and

Lakshmana surrounded by a circle of silent monkey generals.

"Lord Protector of Men save Raama!" cried Seeta.

No sooner had the words left her lips than the clouds burst with the hum of powerful wings. It was none other than the fantastic bird on which the Lord Protector of Men flew through the seven heavens.

All fighting stopped at this sight. Monkeys and demons put down their weapons and stared up at the sky. Raavana, Indrajit and their generals watched from the palace walls. The bird landed beside Raama and grabbed the Serpent Darts in its sharp beak and bronze claws. The snakes squirmed and hissed and shrivelled away. Raama stirred, shaking the cover of death from his body.

He looked at the limp body of Lakshmana beside him in the dust, at the ring of soldiers around him with worried expressions on their faces. He turned to the shining bird and said: *"I feel as if I know you; but I am not sure."*

"My Lord," said the bird, *"you know me well. I look forward to being united with you very soon and we can continue our adventures together once again. For now my work is complete — you and your brother are alive."*

The wonderful bird drew itself up to its full height and flapped its golden wings, sending clouds of dust into the sky. The monkeys covered their eyes as the bird slowly rose higher and higher, till it was a mere speck in the clouds.

"Raama is alive!" shouted Hanumaan. *"Long live Raama and Lakshmana!"* His cry was taken up by the others and the chanting carried all the way to Raavana's palace.

"Can nothing stop this man?" screamed Raavana. *"Tomorrow I will show you all how a true warrior fights. Now leave me all of you. I need to gather my strength for dawn."*

RAAVANA HAD LITTLE REST THAT NIGHT. The first red rays of the morning sun found him tossing among crumpled silk sheets, his mind swimming with the faces of Raama and Seeta, Seeta and Raama . . .

"I feel that you have had enough of the story for the night," said the children's father. "And even if you haven't, I have."

The children rose without a word. "Thanks Dad," said the boy. The girl gave him a kiss on the cheek. The children left the room in silence.

"What's got into them?" said their father. "The story wasn't that bad, was it?"

His wife smiled. "It was wonderful to hear you tell your stories again."

Day 20
The battle continues

SATURDAY ARRIVED. It was a day when the family were all together. The children behaved as if nothing strange had happened, but their hearts were bursting with unanswered questions: Where was Hanumaan? How did their father know the story? Had their father met Hanumaan? Why was the wind so still? Why were their minds on fire, yet their behaviour so cool? Why were they so happy?

Their father watched them go about their tasks with unusual grace and care. "I thought we could continue the story after lunch," he said.

"Yes please," said the children.

"Yes please," said their mother. The girl grinned at her.

Preparations for lunch went swiftly. In fact they had a picnic in the garden. Apart from the wasps that buzzed around the honey pot and dangerously close to ears, it was a very happy lunch. "It's great when we all do this together," said the boy.

"What will be really great is if you help clear away these plates," said his mother.

The girl was alone with her father for a while. "Do you know Hanumaan?" she asked.

Her father didn't move. "Of course I do," he said. "He's in the story."

The girl pinned him to the ground and sat across his belly. "You know what I mean," she said.

Her father sat up slowly and looked her straight in the eyes. "I think I know what you mean . . ." he said. "I do know Hanumaan." His eyes were deep. The girl felt a tiny shiver down her spine.

"You are my Dad, aren't you?" she said.

"I always will be," said her father. "Now if you don't get off my stomach, I won't be able to breath. Here come the others."

They all settled down and the story continued . . .

RAAVANA LED THE NIGHT RANGERS into battle the next day. Raama watched the magnificent golden chariot of the Lord of the Dark Force scattering monkeys and bears to the left and to the right in a terrible trail of blood. Then a solitary monkey leapt onto Raavana's horses, pulling them to the ground and knocking over the chariot. It was Hanumaan. With joined palms the great monkey bowed to Raavana and then delivered him a mighty whack across the chest sending him tumbling in the dust.

A cheer went up from the monkey army. The two warriors fought like gods, sometimes one winning, sometimes the other. Raavana's arrows tore through Hanumaan's flesh, but the monkey just laughed and snapped the shafts in half. He smashed Raavana down with his powerful fists and the demon king's eyes flared up red with anger. Hanumaan could not keep him down.

From a corner of the battlefield Lakshmana saw Hanumaan's plight and rushed to take up the fight. But even his bravery was no match for Raavana's power. Soon he was knocked down unconscious. This was too much for Raama. He climbed on to Hanumaan's shoulders and attacked the Lord of the Dark Force with such power and fury that Raavana didn't know where to turn.

Raavana hurled a flaming spear at Raama, but it was shattered to dust in mid-flight by one of Raama's arrows. Then Raama sent a crescent shaped dart towards Raavana's head, splintering his golden crown into a thousand tiny pieces. This was followed by a thunderbolt weapon which hit Raavana in the chest knocking him to the ground. Raama raised his spear for the kill . . . But then put it down.

"You have fought well today," he said. *"I won't kill you now,*

*not when you still have hundreds of children left to take your
place. I want you to watch me kill all of them. And all of your
brothers too."*

RAAVANA RETURNED TO HIS PALACE defeated. But
soon his fury burst out again. He ordered his guards to go to
the home of his brother, the sleeping giant, and wake him.
The soldiers quaked in fear because everyone knew what
happened when the sleeping giant was aroused — he was bad
tempered and, even worse than that, he was always hungry
and ate anything he could get his hands on.

The soldiers, not wanting to end up as the giant's dinner,
filled a huge cart with bread and rice, meat and wine and
twenty vats of blood. Banging drums and gongs, they entered
the sleeping giant's house. They made a huge commotion,
but still the sleeping giant snored on. They jumped up and
down on his belly and tore at his hair and finally he stirred
and wiped the sleep from his eyes like a baby.

But, once he was fully awake, his anger flared up. He fell
on the cart of food and ate greedily making disgusting
slurping noises. He finished off by eating the two mules that
pulled the cart. The trembling soldiers told him of the battle
that was raging all around and that his brother Raavana had
sent for him.

The giant burst into Raavana's chamber. *"I hear that
the man whose wife you stole is killing our people. Why do you
not take the advice of those around you and give up the
woman?"*

Raavana was stung by these words. *"That man has killed
our brothers in the forest. He has slain thousands of our friends.
He has cut down many of my sons. Shouldn't he be stopped? You*

are the mightiest warrior in the kingdom. I know that you have love for me. Go out and fight."

That's exactly what the sleeping giant did. Once roused, his strength knew no bounds. Like a small mountain he crushed the soldiers of Raama's army. Monkeys and bears scattered at his approach. The monkey generals tried to calm the soldiers down but they too were no match for the giant. Finally Sugreeva himself leapt into battle, but was knocked unconscious by the giant, who then picked him up and carried him though the town to the cheers of the women. They scattered flowers and scented water over their hero. The refreshing droplets fell over Sugreeva too, reviving him. With one jump he was free.

This enraged the giant so much that, uttering a ferocious roar, he waded back into the monkey army, knocking them to the ground and devouring them. Raama's arrows pierced the terrible creature who was covered in blood but still going strong. Finally Raama had had enough. He called out the secret name of one of the explosive weapons. It flashed into his hand. Raama hurled it at the giant and it blew the giant's head off.

When Raavana heard the news of the giant's death it was as if his own head had been blown off. He fell to the floor in a faint. He was comforted by his son Indrajit, who had never been defeated in battle, who promised to put an end to Raama once and for all. He gathered together fresh troops and stormed down on Raama's army like the God of Death. Thousands were killed by this valiant prince of the Dark Force.

Raama and Lakshmana stood together watching with admiration as Indrajit displayed his fantastic skills as a

warrior. Then Raama said: *"Enough of this."* The two
brothers, mounted on bears, charged at Indrajit's chariot. But
the prince of the Dark Force saw them coming and drove his
chariot straight upwards into the clouds where he became
invisible. And from his invisible chariot came a downpour of
such powerful weapons that the battlefield was suddenly
silent. Nothing moved. Then rising from the silence was the
buzz of a fly. Everyone around was dead — even the princes
of Ayodhya.

News reached Hanumaan, Sugreeva and the king of the
bears who were fighting in different corners of the
battlefield. They rushed over to try to help, but saw it was
too late. Raama was dead. Lakshmana was dead. Thousands
of monkeys and bears lay dead.

Raavana appeared on the battlements of his palace and
announced: *"Raama and his brother are dead. Victory is in our
grasp! Tomorrow we shall destroy the rest!"* The city of Lanka
burst into celebration. *"Raama is dead!"* went out the cry.
From her garden prison Seeta heard the cry and fell to her
knees, sobbing violently. Nothing could console her.

But all was not to end this way . . .

THE KING OF THE BEARS, a wise creature, knew of
secret herbs that grew on a particular mountain peak in the
Himalayas. He took Hanumaan to one side and described to
him exactly what the herbs looked like. Hanumaan wasted
little time. Drawing together all his strength he lifted off like
a dart into the blue sky and landed on the medicine
mountain. He searched all over for the herbs he'd been told
about, but they weren't to be seen.

"*I have no time to play silly games with you,*" he said to the mountain and, growing to his full size, he tore the mountain from the earth, heaved it onto his shoulder and leapt back to Lanka. Thoroughly chastened, the mountain revealed its herbs. The wise bear ground the herbs into paste and covered the bodies of the dead warriors with it. Soon the magical properties revived, nourished and fully restored them.

Hanumaan was the hero of the day. From Raavana's palace they could hear the yelps of rejoicing from the monkey camp and fear entered their hearts.

"*What is there to celebrate when Raama is dead?*" cried Raavana. And when his spies brought him the news that

Raama was alive once more, he screamed: *"Is there no end to this man?"*

Soon the smell of burning entered the room. Raavana rushed on to the balcony and saw Lanka in flames again. Sugreeva's soldiers, acting under his orders, had entered the city with flaming torches and set fire to the houses, destroying thousands of them.

More battles followed this, more killing. On the one side was Raavana, stuck to his evil ways, and on the other side there was Raama, prepared to wipe the Dark Force from the face of the earth.

WAR MAKES HEROES and Indrajit was Raavana's hero in the battle for Lanka. It seemed as if his power knew no limit. But there was a limit . . .

Raavana's good brother, Vibeeshana, knew the secret of Indrajit's strength. He took Lakshmana to one side and whispered: *"Indrajit's strength comes from two boons he recieved from the Lord of Creation. The first is that, each time he offered a sacrifice to the Lord before battle, he would be victorious. And the second is, each time he flew into the clouds he would become invisible."*

"Is there no stopping him?" asked Lakshmana.

"There is," said Vibeeshana. *"The boon will fail if Indrajit does not complete the offering to the Lord. Look, there he goes now — to the secret place among the trees. Quick, stop him."*

Hanumaan said: *"Climb onto my shoulders."*

When Lakshmana had mounted, Hanumaan leapt. They landed at the place where Indrajit was making his offering for power. In a flash Hanumaan was on the altar, stamping out the holy fire and scattering the flowers and fruit on the ground. Lakshmana sent an arrow flying towards Indrajit's chariot. It burst into flames.

"Now there is no escape into the clouds, you cheat," said Lakshmana. *"You have destroyed many fine warriors by trickery. Let's see what you can do now that you have no magic on your side."*

A fierce battle followed. Supernatural weapons of thunder, wizards, lightning, filled the sky with strange green and purple lights as they clashed and shattered. Finally Lakshmana called the name of the weapon of the King of the Gods — the Indra-astra. It appeared in his hands, stinking of death. Indrajit trembled with fear at the sight of this deadly shaft. It flew through the air towards him. His head rolled off.

The heavens opened up and the gods showered healing flowers down on Lakshmana, soothing his wounds, singing his praises. *"Excellent! Excellent!"* they cried. Hanumaan lifted the tired Lakshmana onto his shoulders and carried him back to camp. News had already reached Raama who held his brother in his arms.

"Prepare him a bed," said Raama. *"Tomorrow will be the final day."*

"Tomorrow will be the final day," said the children's father. They slept that night among the angels.

Last day
Winning the peace

SUNDAY STARTED GENTLY. The girl was awake early enough to hear the dawn chorus start up — first one or two birds twittering to the sun, then more till, finally, the morning air was a symphony of pure delight. Early as it was, she found her father in the kitchen with a mug of tea and a book.

"You're up early," he said.

"Today's the last day, isn't it?" she said.

"I hope so," said her father. "Why don't you sit quietly and think of Seeta."

The girl shut her eyes and pictures started to rise, one after the other. Seeta alone in the Ashoka Garden. The smell of death overpowering the perfume of the flowers. Pillars of smoke swallowing the sun. Raama nearby, in her heart where she had always seen him, and on the battlefield, destroying her captors.

The girl knew what Seeta was feeling. There was fear alright, but it didn't consume her. There was trembling for certain, but it wasn't going to shake her body to pieces. There was yearning to see the face of her husband and yet a steady knowledge that she had never been without him.

The girl heard her father's voice: "Would you like some tea?" he asked.

She blinked and shook the dream from her head. "Yes please."

"You realise," he said, "that the last part of this story needs to be told at sunset."

She nodded.

The children couldn't wait for the day to pass. Eventually the sun drifted down and the sky turned red. The children settled themselves for the final story . . .

RAAMA LOOKED OVER THE BATTLEFIELD. There was something clean about the morning. The red earth of

Lanka had been cleared of bodies. A lone horse limped across the field, fully saddled and bridled, searching for its master. A hawk rode the high currents of wind, drifting in wide circles, keeping balance with only tiny flicks of the tips of its wing feathers.

Raama called together the leaders of the monkey army. *"This fight has been a terrifying one. We have lost friends to the Lord of Death. We have dispatched countless enemies into his jaws. Remember this story and tell it to your grandchildren. Tell them how you fought beside Raama against the power of the Dark Force. Tell them for the sake of inspiration. Tell them for the sake of encouragement. Today Raama and Seeta will be united once more. Now go and stir the blood of war in your troops."*

The battle started with a terrible clash. Both sides, sensing the end was near, put their hearts into the fight as never before and once more the field of Lanka was littered with the bodies and limbs of dead warriors. Several of Raavana's sons met their death that morning and several great monkey heroes too.

Raama was finally ready. He mounted Hanumaan's shoulder and twanged his bow. The sound sent shivers through the hearts of all who heard it. It brought joy to Seeta. It raised anger in Raavana. He called for his chariot and armour and was soon cutting swathes through the monkey army.

"He's magnificent," said Raama to Hanumaan.

"But he must die," came back Hanumaan's stern reply.

"Let it be so," said Raama. *"Get me to him."*

Hanumaan leapt high above the heads of the soldiers and landed with a deep thud right in front of Raavana's chariot.

Raavana's horses reared up and came to a dead stop. Raama and Raavana eyed one another.

Raavana smiled. *"I have imagined this moment for a long time. Salutations to you."*

Raama replied: *"Give up Seeta and surrender to me."*

Raavana smiled again. *"You know that is impossible."*

"Then let what will be, be," said Raama.

"How can it be otherwise?" said Raavana.

The two warriors bowed to one another and took their places for battle. The start was quick and fierce. Weapons shattered weapons, flights of arrows swarmed like hornets from bows. Spears, clubs, shafts, darts exploded in flames and thunder.

Finally Raama called: *"Brahmaa-astra, destroyer of foes, undefeated of all heavenly weapons, I have need of your power."* The awesome weapon, dripping with the blood and rotting flesh of evil doers, appeared beside the Lord Prince of Ayodhya. It bowed to him and, in a mighty explosion, burst into flight.

Raavana watched. Brave. Calm. A true warrior facing the moment of his death. The Brahmaa-astra struck him in the chest and exploded through the other side. *"All majesty to you Lord Raama, for I am released,"* cried Raavana and he fell to the dust of the battlefield, dead.

The heavens opened. Flowers showered down. A sweet, scented rain washed away the fire and revived the many thousand monkeys and bears that had been killed in battle.

IMAGINE THE CELEBRATION that followed. Hanumaan was sent to carry the joyful news to Seeta. Raama was carried by a jubilant Sugreeva through the gates of the fortress city. His first job was to announce that Lanka had a new ruler — Vibeeshana, the good brother of Raavana.

Tens of thousands of monkeys and bears lined the path that led from the Ashoka Garden to the palace. Suddenly a flock of white birds lifted off from the trees of the garden. A ripple of excitement spread through the crowd. From the palace steps they could hear that Seeta was approaching.

When Raama's eyes finally fell on her face, his heart sang with bliss. She looked splendid in fresh clothes and jewels, walking with the slight swinging gait of an imperial elephant, eyes cast down, each footstep steady.

"You have sent for me, my Lord," she said without lifting her eyes.

"Daughter of Janaka, there is one more ordeal before we can be joined once again. Painful though it must be, I need to ask in the presence of all these witnesses: Have you remained pure during your months in this kingdom?" Raama's voice was firm and unwavering. It was shocking in its bluntness.

Seeta heard the words as if being hit by lightning. She rocked for a moment. Sugreeva moved to steady her, but she regained her balance. Only Raama hadn't stirred an inch.

Seeta said: *"To prove that I have been pure during these long and unhappy months of separation, I will call upon the Lord of Fire as my witness. Prepare the largest bonfire you can manage. Let its flames be so high that they are visible throughout this land. Seeta is pure."*

Raama nodded. Hanumaan directed the monkeys in building the fire. They cut down tall trees and piled the logs high. They poured oil over the pyre and set it alight.

Seeta walked steadily towards the flames and entered them. Few people in the crowd fell to the floor in shock. Others

lowered their eyes in shame. Raama did not move. Then he
stood and, after what seemed an eternity, called: *"Enough!"*

The flames parted — and everyone around witnessed that
they had been observing the cape of the Lord of Fire,
wrapped around Seeta to protect her.

She lifted her eyes and met Raama's. They were smiling.
"I never had any doubts," he whispered. *"The trial was for the
people's sake. Now they can never say that Raama, blinded by his
love, placed an impure lady on the throne."*

Hanumaan led Seeta to her husband and all his friends. At
that very moment a gong sounded from the throne room.
Hanumaan appeared at the top of the steps. *"That sound was
the beat of time. Fourteen years in exile came to an end at that
very instant."*

"Time to go home," said Raama. The prince took his
goddess by the hand.

From above the heads of the crowd came the sound of
fluttering wings. The celestial chariot, glinting gold, drawn
by swans, appeared before them. Raama, Seeta and
Lakshmana stepped into it amidst wild cheering and clapping
and fireworks.

"Someone's missing," said Raama. He searched the faces of
the crowd and then spotted him. *"Hanumaan, Son of the Lord
of the Wind, would you join us in Ayodhya?"*

"My heart sings to hear your words," said Hanumaan.
*"Nothing would please me more than to continue to serve
Raama."* He stepped up into the chariot. The wings of the
swans slowly started to flap their rhythm. The chariot started
to roll forward and steadily its wheels left the ground. They
circled the kingdom and turned North, heading straight for
Ayodhya.

The children were very still and very happy. Their father was beaming, their mother laughing her laugh that they all so loved, rocking back and forth.

"Did Hanumaan tell you the story?" asked the boy. "And give you oranges?"

"He told me that he was waiting for a special moment to tell the *whole* story, to special people — I think he was waiting for you," said their father. "He only told me about the battle..."

The boy interrupted: "What I can't understand is why Raavana said: 'All Majesty to you, Lord Raama'. Wasn't Raama his enemy?"

His father smiled. "The Lord of the Dark Force knows he can never win in the end. Only Raama was strong enough to set him free from his wickedness and that was all he wanted."

The girl looked straight at her father. "What of Hanumaan?" she asked.

"Hanumaan is alive and well," said her father, "the force of reason fighting on the side of love and honour. We just have to call him. He lives in each of us."

"Are you Hanumaan?" asked the boy.

"I am your father," said their father.

"Do you know Hanumaan well?" asked the girl.

"I most certainly do," came the reply.

"How did you meet?" asked the boy.

"It was on a day, pretty much like this one, only warmer, that I went to play in the park with my friends. I left them behind and hid in a secret grove of poplars that only I knew," their father said. "That's where I first met Hanumaan."

A gentle breeze started to blow. It kissed their cheeks and ruffled their hair. The children smiled at their father. He winked back.